SEA GLASS SUMMER

RACHEL HANNA

PROLOGUE

Tara Lawson was eleven years old and had a heart full of dreams. This morning, she walked along the beach, her eyes searching the sand for sea glass, as she always did. Beside her was Noah, her ever-present best friend and partner in this treasure hunt.

They each moved along with the same intent to find the best sea glass on the beach that morning. It was something they did as many days of the week as they could. The early morning sun painted the beach in shades of gold and pink, creating a world that felt like it belonged only to them.

As they walked along, Tara couldn't help but look over at Noah. He had been her friend since third grade, but lately she found herself thinking about him differently. Her grandmother said it was just because she was growing up, and she might be more interested in boys, but she wasn't interested in any boys except for Noah.

Of course, he had no idea. He was oblivious, like most boys. She wondered if he ever thought about her that way, too. But, in the quiet of the morning with the sound of just the waves and the seagulls, it felt safe to have these personal thoughts that she could keep to herself. They were like whispers lost on the sea breeze.

They methodically searched the beach, something they had perfected over many countless mornings. Tara loved these moments. The beach was her favorite place. It made her feel safe and secure in a world that wasn't always that way.

The cool sand was under her feet, and Noah's easy presence was beside her. Seagrove was comforting to her, and it was a place that even in her eleven-year-old little heart she cherished deeply. Suddenly, Noah's voice broke through her daydreaming.

"Tara, look!" he exclaimed. He held up a shard of green sea glass. Noah's smile was infectious. She couldn't help but smile back and felt her heart flutter a little. Was that normal?

"You always find the best pieces," she said, admiring him, but feeling jealous at the same time.

They continued their search as Tara's mind wandered to a future she often thought about. It was unusual for a girl her age. She knew that, but she couldn't help it. She wondered if there would be a day where she and Noah might be more than friends. Maybe they would go to homecoming or prom together, and then maybe one day they would live by this very stretch of beach teaching their own kids about finding sea glass. The thoughts made her heart swell in a way she wasn't familiar with, but she liked it. One time, she'd picked up her teacher's romance novel that she hid in her desk drawer and read a scene where the hunky man on the cover kissed the woman in the story. That gave her a little tingle, but nothing like thinking about Noah did.

As they reached their favorite spot on the beach where the waves were gently lapping the shore, Tara saw something half buried near a cluster of rocks. It was a piece of blue sea glass, which was beautiful and rare. She ran over to pick it up, turning it over in her fingers. It felt like a sign, a secret message from the sea only meant for her.

"Wow, Tara. That one's amazing," Noah said as he came over to look.

3

For a moment, their hands brushed as he took the sea glass from her so he could examine it. She felt a warmth spread through her for a moment, and she wondered if Noah felt it, too. They sat down on the sand and looked at their collection of the day's sea glass spread out before them. It was almost time to get ready for school.

Most kids were probably still in bed or eating breakfast, but they always figured out how to get to the beach together to look for their beloved sea glass. Tara looked at Noah, his face lit by the soft morning light, and she felt a sense of belonging. She would always have Noah. She was sure of that. This was where she was meant to be - with her best friend sitting beside her, surrounded by an endless ocean. After a few minutes, they packed up their treasures and headed to each of their houses, Tara making a silent promise to herself to always hold on to this feeling and maybe, just maybe, her dreams of a beautiful future by the ocean weren't so farfetched.

CHAPTER 1

*T*ara Lawson had always been successful. Even in school as a kid, she was the teacher's pet, always striving to do the right things. That extended to college, where she was a member of the journalism club, wrote for the school newspaper, and interned at a local TV news station.

Sometimes, she thought maybe it was because she lost her parents so young. Her father had died in a motorcycle accident when she was just a toddler, and her mother had passed away from a brain tumor just before she was to start third grade in the south Georgia town where they lived at the time. Her early life had been plagued with death and sadness, and the only thing she'd known to do was work hard and impress the adults around her.

When she'd gone to live with her grandmother

in Seagrove, South Carolina, she'd had a whole new set of teachers to impress, and impress them she did. She even became her high school's valedictorian before applying to colleges. She got into all of them. In the end, she chose The University of Georgia, where she got her degree in Journalism.

Now thirty years old, she stood in the office of her boss, Mack Valentine. She'd been working as a producer for a popular TV news show in Atlanta for about three years now. Today was, by far, her worst day on the job. The blunder she'd made was major, and her heart pounded as she waited for Mack to join her in his office.

She stared at his Emmy awards lining the bookshelf across from his desk. None of them even had so much as a fingerprint on them, and she was sure he shined them regularly. Mack was a stickler for everything. Not a hair out of place. Not a crooked paper on his desk. Not even a piece of trash in his fancy stainless steel garbage can. It was probably just for looks.

He was a major figure in the TV news industry, and getting this job had been her big dream for so many years. She was sure she could talk her way out of this. Maybe she could explain how her recent shocking breakup with her fiancé of two years had caused her to have a temporary brain hiccup.

The problem was, she knew Mack Valentine wouldn't care. He was a harsh man, to say the least. He ran a tight ship; he knew everybody in the news business, and the last time she'd seen him - thirty minutes ago - his face was so red she thought it might explode.

As she stared out the window over the Atlanta skyline, she heard the door open behind her. Feeling like she was in slow motion, she turned to face him.

"Mack, I'm so sorry..." she said, holding up her newly manicured hands. Mack said he didn't want to see any un-manicured hands on his show, and that included the men.

He held up his hand, which was also quite well kept. "Stop."

Tara bit her lip and stood there, her stomach churning. "Okay."

He walked around her and sat down at his desk, pointing at one of the plush leather chairs across from him. "Sit."

Like a Golden Retriever, she sat on command, staring at her hands in her lap. She saw a spot on her index fingernail where her new pale pink polish was missing, so she hid it under another, better-looking finger.

Tara was no shrinking violet. She'd interviewed all kinds of people in her career, from politicians to prisoners. She didn't usually get intimidated by people, except for Mack Valentine.

"Mack, if you'll just let me explain how all this happened..."

"Do you really think that matters, Tara? Because I don't."

"I thought my source was credible. You know I always do good work. But, I wanted to get the story to air as quickly as I could. I know how you hate when WTBZ gets the scoop on us."

He shook his head. "Not when the story is fake!" Tara jumped when he yelled, her heart flipping over in her chest. Mack regularly got upset about things, but she'd never seen him like this.

"I didn't know that."

"Tara, there's no way you vetted this source enough before going to air. You had our top anchor read a story saying that Dan Altman, one of this state's most prominent politicians, covered up a contaminated water system in one of our most populated counties!"

"We both know Dan Altman would do something like that, Mack. He's corrupt, through and through."

"We're journalists, Tara. We don't get to make determinations on a person's character and craft stories around it."

"I didn't *craft* a story! You know that. I do good work. I just messed up vetting this source. I should've done more. I admit that." She wanted to tell him she'd been up all night crying over her failed engagement, thinking about all her mess ups in the last few years. Missing her mom and dad, even though she didn't remember her dad. She just missed *having* a dad. What would it be like right now to call a parent who loved her unconditionally and get advice? She would never know.

He stared at her. "I don't know how we're going to get out of this mess, but I do know that I can't keep you here, Tara."

She looked at him, her mouth slightly hanging open. "What are you saying? I've been here for three years. Surely one mistake will not cause you to fire me?"

He stood up, leaning over the desk. "This wasn't one little mistake. This is something that is going to take weeks to undo, and could cost us all kinds of money to litigate. I know Dan Altman, and he's probably going to sue us for this fake story."

"Please, Mack, you can't do this to me. I didn't do this intentionally. I'll talk to Dan Altman myself."

He shook his head. "No, that's not going to work. And you know you've made a series of errors in the last few months. I don't know what's going on with you, but we can't have that here. I just can't allow it anymore. I've tried to give you space to figure out whatever is going on in your life, but it's bleeding over into your work, and now it's potentially going to cost us a lot of money. I can't keep you here. I'm sorry."

She felt the color draining from her face as she sat frozen in the chair across from him. Surely she was dreaming this. Without him noticing, she reached over and pinched her own arm. Yep, that hurt. All of this hurt.

"I don't know what I'm going to do," she said, not really asking a question. It was more of a vocalized existential crisis comment. Mack didn't respond. A few moments of silence passed between them before she stood up slowly. "I want you to know I really appreciate the time that I got to work here. It was a big dream of mine to work with you."

"Tara, I think you should take some time off from

the industry." That was his response? After she gave him that compliment, that was what he said? It made her heart skip a beat. She was surprised her heart wasn't going into full-blown fibrillation with this stress.

He didn't tell her she was a talented journalist and she would get through this. He didn't tell her he would hire her back once she got herself together, or that he would give her a reference somewhere else. He told her to *take time off*. That wasn't what she expected to hear.

Without saying another word, Tara turned around and walked out of his office, quietly closing the door behind her. She walked toward her cubicle, people speaking to her in the hallway along the way, but she couldn't form any words. That was lovely. A journalist who couldn't form words.

She sat down at her desk and started opening the drawers, mindlessly taking her personal effects and shoving them into the tote bag she brought with her every day. Thankfully, she didn't have a lot on her desk. She didn't have pictures of a husband and kids. She didn't even have a dog. She just had a couple of little personal effects and a bag of nuts in her drawer. Once she shoved everything into the bag, she got up and walked toward the door. Again, people were talking to her, asking her where she was going, if she was okay. She said nothing, and instead walked silently out onto the streets of Atlanta, staring up at the skyscrapers as she made her way to the parking garage, where she parked her car every day.

There were so many things she was going to miss about working in the city, and she hoped to get back there soon. She didn't know if she would be able to even get another job. Everybody knew Mack Valentine, and he was sure to pass the word around that she was not somebody to be hired. She passed by her favorite coffee shop and wondered when she would go in there again to get a caramel latte. She passed by the place where she took her dry cleaning and wondered if Bob, the owner, would wonder where she was when she didn't show up with an arm full of pantsuits next week. And then the cafe where she got her sandwich every day at lunch. Would they wonder why she wasn't coming in to order her chicken salad croissant with extra chopped up bread and butter pickles? Tara liked the monotony of it all. She enjoyed knowing that she had a place to go, a place where she fit in. Right now, she felt like the entire world was about to hate her, and she had no idea what to do about it.

J ulie sat on the front porch of her home staring at the mailbox. She'd been out here for fifteen minutes wondering where her mailman, Peter, was this morning. He always delivered the mail no later than 11:30 AM, and she only had limited time before she had to get to the bookstore. Thankfully, Meg was taking the morning shift, so she had a bit of extra time.

She was home alone, with Dawson out working on a contracting job and Dylan at school. Of course, she wouldn't want her family to see her doing this, the thing that she did every day now. If they knew what she had been up to, they would have a lot of questions and she had no answers.

She felt very vulnerable about the whole thing, and she kind of wished she hadn't even started it. She continued staring at the mailbox, willing the mailman to show up. Every day had been the same for the last few weeks - wait for the mail to come, feel disappointed, and then go to work.

That was pretty much her life now, and she was having a hard time hiding it from Dawson, especially. He was her husband, her biggest supporter, the man she'd loved most in her whole life. And yet she just couldn't tell him about this. It was too embarrassing.

Finally, she heard the tires of the postal truck coming down the gravel road. She stood up and plodded toward the mailbox, waving her hand and forcing a smile.

"Hey there, Julie," Peter called, as he usually did. He was a young man, but very much on time, which was something Julie appreciated. It was almost 11:30 after all, and she needed to force down an early lunch before getting to the bookstore.

"Good morning. Have anything interesting for me today?"

He walked over and handed her a stack of mail. An Amazon package, a couple of bills, and another envelope she couldn't identify. "Just a few things today."

"Well, thanks. Hope you have a good rest of your route," she said, waving at him as he climbed back into the truck.

She walked up to the porch and laid everything beside her, searching through the stack for the envelope she didn't recognize. When she opened it and read it, she felt her stomach churn. It wasn't good news. It was never good news.

T ara sat in her apartment as she had been doing for the last several days. She watched trashy TV, ate bags of chips one after the other, and tried to contemplate what she was going to do with the rest of her life. At thirty years old, it was all over, it seemed. That journalism degree was just as worthless as a coupon that expired yesterday. She hadn't applied for any jobs, and she had thought about dipping into her savings just to pay the rent for a couple of months while she got back on her feet.

Maybe she would get involved in one of those MLM companies like some of her friends had done. Sell make-up or cooking supplies or essential oils at home parties and try to recruit her friends to do the same. The thought made her laugh. She didn't have enough friends for that, anyway.

She had also spent a lot of time trying not to text her ex-fiancé. Not that she was madly in love with him and wanted to hear his voice. It was that she wanted something to ground her, to root her in reality. The only other family member she had living was her grandmother back in Seagrove, South Carolina. She wanted to call her, but she was too embarrassed. She would call her this Sunday, as she always did, just to check on her and make sure she was okay. That was only a couple of days away, and already she was dreading it.

She adored her grandmother. The woman had raised her and had been the only mother she had really ever known, given that hers had died when she was in elementary school. But she didn't want to disappoint her. She didn't want to tell her how she had screwed up so big that she had lost her entire career in one fell swoop.

She decided she had to do something productive today. Maybe a little grocery shopping or a little online shopping, anything to get her mind off how her life had gone off the rails. Maybe she'd tackle her junk drawer or clean out her closet. More than likely, she'd pull everything out of her closet and sit in the middle of an unfinished mess in a few hours while she sat on her floor scrolling social media and crying.

She decided it was good to first take a shower, so she didn't scare anybody in public. As she stood up and headed toward her bedroom to get something to wear, her cell phone buzzed in her pocket. Maybe that was Mack Valentine calling to ask her to come back. He couldn't do the news without her. The station was falling apart. Yeah, that was realistic.

"Hello?" she said, leaning against her bedroom doorframe.

"Is this Tara Lawson?" a woman's voice asked on the other end of the phone. She sounded very official. Maybe it was an attorney calling to tell her she was being sued for the fake story that she had inadvertently produced.

"This is she," Tara said, cautiously.

"Tara, this is Anita Wilcox. I'm an attorney in Seagrove, South Carolina."

An attorney in Seagrove? Why would she be calling her? Certainly she wouldn't handle a case for somebody in Atlanta. That would be an awfully coincidental thing to happen.

"Okay..." Tara said, still not understanding why this woman was calling her.

"I don't quite know how to say this, but your grandmother passed away this morning, and I'm her attorney."

"Excuse me, what?" Tara said, as if she didn't understand what was being said.

"I figured someone would have called you from the funeral home already."

"Nobody called me," Tara said, still not believing what this woman was saying. This had to be some kind of prank call. Her grandmother was in great health. "I don't understand…"

"I know this might be shocking news. I understand your grandmother raised you, because she spoke of you often when we would meet."

"You're saying that my grandmother died?" Tara asked, confused. It was like her brain couldn't accept the information and just kept spitting it back out.

"Yes, she passed away peacefully in her sleep."

Tara leaned harder against the doorframe, willing it to hold her body upright. She felt like her knees were going to give way.

"But there has to be some mistake," she said, tears welling in her eyes.

"Honey, I know this has to be a shocking phone call to get, but there is no mistake. I need you to come to Seagrove to help settle your grandmother's estate."

Tara heard very little else of what the woman said. She gave her other details that were probably important, but she would have to call back to again to get the details because she couldn't think straight. Her life had spiraled, and it seemed like nothing was in her control anymore.

Colleen was dead on her feet. Being a new mother was the hardest job she had ever done. Forget all those crazy jobs she did in high school or the legal work she did before coming to Seagrove. Forget working in the toy business with Tucker. All of that paled in comparison to how hard it was to get anything done with no sleep.

Of course, if she would ask for help, she would definitely get it. Her family and friends would rally around her which would make her feel like a complete imbecile for not being able to do the thing that nature intended: be a mom. Be a good mom. She wasn't sure she was ever going to be able to do that.

Sitting at home while Tucker was at work just made her feel even more lonely. She adored her new baby boy. Deacon was a wonderful baby, although she had no one to compare him to. But she was just so tired mentally and physically that she wondered if she would ever climb out of it. She supposed that all new moms probably felt this way, especially when it had only been a few weeks since giving birth.

Being a new mom had been the hardest thing she'd ever gone through in her life. She had been thrilled to be having a baby with Tucker, of course. She did all the fun things throughout the year - baby showers, shopping for baby clothes, going to birthing classes, everything you were supposed to do.

But now, as she stood here staring down at baby Deacon's diaper, she found herself assessing what color poop should be. Why was it green? Was he sick with something? Her brain felt like it was a sponge, but not in a good way. Like it was mushy and without any kind of knowledge whatsoever.

Again, she could ask for help. Her mother had been offering since day one. But she wanted to do this by herself. She wanted to have these bonding moments with her new baby boy. Right now, she felt like she could curl up into the fetal position on her sofa and never wake up again. She needed a nap. She needed a *week-long* nap. She never got a full night of sleep. Even when Tucker got up with the baby, which was most nights, Colleen woke up, too. She just couldn't help it.

On top of that, they had gotten a big new account at the toy company and she knew Tucker needed help. Only the two of them worked there. Their last assistant had quit because she was relocating for her husband's job. They needed to hire somebody else.

They needed to do a lot of things. There just wasn't enough time in the day.

She finished changing Deacon's diaper and then went and sat on the sofa, staring at the TV, which wasn't even turned on. She held him close to her and leaned her head back, closing her eyes. She couldn't do that for long, of course, because she didn't want to fall asleep holding him.

Her pregnancy had been pretty uneventful, and she was thankful for that. She hadn't had any major issues, and she had gone exactly to her due date before giving birth. Her labor wasn't even that bad. It only lasted eight hours, which she understood was pretty short, especially for a first pregnancy. There were no complications, and baby Deacon had no issues at birth. All in all, it was a lot to be thankful for.

Even so, she struggled. Sometimes, she wondered if she was suffering from some post-partum baby blues or something like that, or maybe this was just all normal. She tried to read books about it, but she couldn't stay awake long enough to do it. Surely the people around her noticed that she wasn't operating on all cylinders. But every time they offered to help, she refused. It was baffling, even to her.

As she held her baby close and looked down at his perfect little features, Colleen couldn't help but feel a wave of gratitude wash over her. She had a lot to be thankful for, and she was aware of that. So many women couldn't have babies or had lost babies. She would never take this for granted. But she couldn't help but admit to herself that if she didn't get some rest soon, she might just lose her mind.

CHAPTER 2

*A*s Tara drove into Seagrove, so many memories flooded back to her. She'd lived there from the time she was in third grade, all the way up until she left for college. Of course, she had come back to see her grandmother as often as she could, but it got harder over the years as she got busier and busier in her career.

Being a journalist meant that she might be sent out on assignment for days or weeks at a time, and even though she was only working in Atlanta the last few years, it had still become very hard to get home on a regular basis. Still, she constantly stayed in contact with her grandmother. She taught her how to text. Sometimes she emailed her, and they always made sure to have a phone call or a video chat on Sundays. That was typically the day that Tara had the most time free. She would stay home all day, make herself a healthy meal, do her laundry and call her grandma. It was her routine. Now that routine would be no more.

As she drove down the roads in Seagrove onto the town square, so many places made her feel comfortable and at home. The bookstore, the bakery that had only opened recently, and she had eaten at a couple of times on visits home, the dry cleaners, the town library, and even the courthouse. But most of all, when she passed her elementary school, she felt warm flutters in her heart. That was where she had met her best friend. At least he had been her best friend back in those days. It had been years since they had last spoken.

She had fond memories of school because of him. She had been involved in many things throughout her school years. It was the place where she felt like she excelled, where she felt like she fit in. She felt bad for those kids who got bullied or didn't fit in at school. For Tara, it had been a refuge, a rest from the grief that she had struggled with since she was a little kid.

Losing your parents at such a young age, even when you had a loving grandmother to raise you, made you feel adrift, like you're out on the sea in a small little life raft, and you're not tethered to anything in particular. She hated to say that or even think that way because her grandmother had been wonderful. She had stepped up in a way that many people wouldn't have been able to do. Still, Tara had always missed her mom and dad. She didn't remember her father at all, and only had a few fleeting memories of her mother. She had pictures, though, and she kept them with her, on her phone and in frames around her house. She never wanted to forget them.

As she drove down one of the side streets toward her grandmother's house, she felt her stomach clenching into a knot. This wasn't something she wanted to do, yet it was something she had always known would have to be done one day. Her grandmother had seemed invincible, like she would live forever. For her age, she had been in good health, or at least that's what Tara had thought. Maybe something was going on that she wasn't sharing with her on their weekly phone calls. That was entirely possible since her grandmother had always done everything she could to protect her.

She pulled up in front of the house and sucked in a breath, holding it way longer than she probably needed to. For some reason, seeing it, even though she had seen it a million times over her life, made her feel jittery. Uncomfortable. On edge. Instead of feeling welcoming, it felt like she had a huge void in her heart suddenly. She let out the breath before she passed out and turned off the car, looking at the house. It wasn't much. Her grandmother had lived a very simple life. It was a small white cottage-style home on one of the streets near the town square. All the homes on this block were built back in the 1920s.

Her grandmother's house was more of a shotgun style house, narrow at the front, but deep. It had an adorable front porch that had been replaced just a few years ago. There was a swing with fluffy pillows hanging at one end of it. Her grandmother loved to sit out there every evening having a cup of coffee and talking to her neighbors as they walked their dogs. She was beloved in town, and that was one reason Tara felt comfortable not coming home as often as she probably should have. She knew her grandmother had plenty of people watching over her, but she felt that familiar pang of guilt. Maybe she should have come home more often. Maybe her grandmother was struggling with something health-wise that she didn't know about and could have helped her with.

Anytime someone passes away, there's a

tendency for the people left behind to try to figure out what they could have done better. But in the end, she knew her grandmother would say that everybody's name was written on a big scroll in heaven with the date that they would go meet God, and that couldn't be changed. Tara hung onto that because it made her feel better.

She got out of her car and retrieved her two duffel bags from the back seat before walking up to the front door. The attorney had hidden the key under a flowerpot on the porch so that she could get settled, and they would meet in a couple of days about the will. Tara had told her she just wasn't ready to do it yet. She needed a couple of days to decompress, so the attorney had agreed. There was no big hurry. She knew the house had been left to her since she was the only family her grandmother had. It wasn't as if she wasn't going to leave the house to Tara all along. After all, she considered her not only a granddaughter, but a daughter. She walked inside and could have sworn she smelled her grandmother's perfume, a mixture of magnolia blossoms and musk that always signaled that her grandmother was in the room.

She put down her bags in the foyer and walked around slowly, looking at all the places in the house that held memories for her. Pretty much every single room. Every nook and cranny. After all, she'd lived there for most of her life. She walked over and sat down on the sofa in the small living room, staring out the window at the town square just beyond her front yard. It was weird to be back in Seagrove. On one hand, she felt comfortable here. Welcome, like she was at home. It was unlike any other place she'd ever been in her life. But at the same time, she felt grief over losing her grandmother, over losing her career, even over losing her fiancé.

As the weeks had passed, she realized that the relationship hadn't been a good one for her, but at her age, she just wanted to get married and settle down. Maybe it was old-fashioned, but that's how she felt. And now here she was starting all over again. Starting over in her career, or possibly even having to change careers. Starting over in the relationship department and having to do it all alone without her beloved grandmother. Everything seemed so up in the air. For now, the only thing she could think to do was take a nap, so she laid down and curled up, clutching her grandmother's cross-stitch pillow to her chest as she allowed the tears to flow before she dozed off.

O ne of the things that Julie was most grateful for in her life was that she got to own a bookstore. She had loved books since she was a little girl. They were often her respite from difficult times with her family or at school. She loved the escape they provided even now. She was under a lot of stress recently, most of it she didn't want to talk about to her friends and family. She wasn't somebody who liked to bring everybody around her down, and lately she wasn't feeling the most optimistic and positive. She tried to put on a smiley face, and she spent most of her time escaping into books when there were no customers in the store.

As she stood at the shelf filled with self-help books, she toyed with the idea of buying a book to help her get through this difficult time. For most people, this wouldn't have been such a hard time, but for her, she was feeling a wee bit hopeless. Just as she was about to sink into more despair in her mind, Dixie walked in, a sure tonic to her bad mood.

"Good morning, darlin'," Dixie said, her voice booming across the bookstore. The woman was the epitome of larger-than-life.

"Hey there. I thought you had a tennis lesson this morning."

"Oh, I do. He said he'd be running about thirty minutes late, so I thought I'd stop by for a quick chat. How are things going?"

"They're going fine. Business has been good, and we just got a new shipment of books in this morning. Lots to put away," Julie said, trying not to make eye contact. She knew that if she looked at her, Dixie would surely know something was wrong with her. She could peg her easily like that.

"You okay?" Dixie asked, standing in front of her with her hands on her hips. Julie couldn't help but smile when she saw Dixie's little hot pink tennis skirt, her bright white tennis shoes and socks with little balls on the back of them. Dixie was always flamboyantly dressed, whether she was playing tennis or going to church. It didn't matter. She felt like you had to show off your best side when you were out in public.

"I'm fine. Just a little tired is all."

"I suppose you've been helping Colleen with her new situation of being a mom."

"Oh, a little bit. She doesn't really allow people to help her too much. I think she's probably exhausted, but she doesn't want to admit it."

"Well, that does run in your family, I suppose."

Julie looked at her. "What is that supposed to mean?"

Dixie cocked her head to the side. "It means that I know something's wrong with you, but you won't tell me what it is. I've been asking you about it for weeks now. I'm your friend. I hope you know that. You can tell me anything."

She smiled slightly. "I know. It's just something silly that I'm having trouble with, but I'd prefer to keep it to myself. I don't want to bring anybody else down."

"Honey, it's not bringing other people down to share your struggles. They are much easier to carry when you're not carrying them alone."

"I appreciate it. I really do." And she did. She wanted Dixie to know that, but she still didn't want to share what was going on. After all, she hadn't even shared it with Dawson. All of it was embarrassing. Demoralizing. She just didn't want to talk about it, but it was all she could think about.

"Well, if you do change your mind and you want to talk, you know where to find me."

Just as they finished their conversation, Janine came walking in, holding a wiggling Madison in her arms. Madison had just turned a year old, and she had learned to walk a couple of days before. The kid hadn't stopped moving since then. She spent a lot of time at Janine's yoga studio, copying the poses, running around and dancing everywhere.

"Goodness me, that one looks like she has had a couple of espressos this morning," Dixie said laughing. Janine let out a big breath and then put her on the ground, watching her toddle around the bookstore, heading straight for the children's section where there were stuffed animals in a basket in the corner.

"You're telling me. She's a wiggle worm," Janine said laughing, wiping the back of her hand across her forehead. "I need a nap."

"Well, if you ever need a babysitter, I'm happy to help. Although I'm not sure I could keep up with her by myself," Dixie said laughing. "I hate to cut this short, but I guess I better head over to the rec center. I'll see you ladies later," she said waving and smiling as she walked out the door.

Julie was so happy to see that Dixie had finally found something to keep her busy, keep her active, and make her happy. It was a wonderful thing to witness.

"Hey sis. No classes today?" Julie asked as she put some new books up on the shelf.

"Yeah, after lunchtime. I just figured I would take Madison out for a little walk this morning, and I thought we'd stop by and see how you're doing."

Julie shrugged her shoulders. "I'm doing fine. How are you doing?"

Janine stared at her. "I'm your sister. I know something's up. I wish you would tell me what it is."

Julie rolled her eyes inside. "I just got the same lecture from Dixie. I wish y'all would just quit asking me."

"And what kind of sister would I be if I quit asking you?" Janine asked.

"Listen, I appreciate everybody's concern but I'm fine, really. I've just got a little something on my mind, and I'll get through it. I promise. It's nothing to be super worried about."

"Are you sure?"

"I'm sure. I promise if there was something serious going on, I would tell you."

"Well, I just want you to know that you can talk to me. It doesn't matter how small you think it is."

"I know, and I appreciate it."

Just then, they heard a crash as Madison pulled several books off a shelf. Thankfully, none of them hit her, but it scared her enough to make her come running back to her mother.

"I'd better get this one out of here before she destroys the place," Janine said, picking her up and laughing. "Take care of yourself, sis. Okay?"

"I'm fine! Go enjoy your day with your daughter," she said, pinching one of Madison's pudgy little cheeks and forcing a smile. As she watched them leave and walk down the sidewalk, Julie sighed. She had to get her mind right before all her friends and family had an intervention with her.

Tara sat in the living room of her grandmother's home, almost frozen in place. She'd been looking at pictures most of the day, finding boxes of them tucked away in different areas of the home. Her grandmother loved old photos. She enjoyed reminiscing about the past. As she sat there in the middle of an ocean of memories scattered across the table in front of her, she could see little dust particles dancing in the air, shimmering like little stars in the fading sunlight that was coming through the old windows.

She picked up one of the older photo albums that she had already looked through a couple of times, its cover marked up after years of use. She turned each page carefully and stepped back in time through a vivid journey of her family.

She stopped on a photograph of her and Noah, her childhood best friend. It had been so many years since she had seen him. In this moment, they were perched on the creaky front porch of her grandmother's house, their faces showing wide grins with ice cream staining their chins and shirts. She remembered that carefree time in her life when she was a kid. Why was being an adult so much harder?

She ran her finger over Noah's face, looking at his impish eyes that twinkled with such mischief back then. They hadn't seen each other in so long that she wondered what he was doing now, what he looked like. Did he get married? Did he have kids? All of their choices had led them further and further apart since high school. A deep ache of nostalgia filled her. Noah had been her very best friend in the world. They had been on countless adventures around Seagrove. He knew most of her dreams and all of her fears. It was something to have a best friend like that, and she couldn't believe that she had let it go. It hadn't been on purpose. Just life, the thing that happens to most people.

She continued diving through the photo albums, looking at pictures of her parents which captured forever their youthful excitement and smiles. It was a bittersweet picture of what her life could have been if they had both lived longer. Her heart clenched in her chest as she held an image of her mother, whose smile came through with such warmth and affection that she felt like she was really in the room. The older she got, the more Tara's memories were fading of her parents. So when she looked at pictures it brought them back, even if just for a moment. Sometimes she felt terrible that she couldn't remember her mother's voice anymore. After all, she had been pretty young when her mother had passed away. For years, she could hear it in her mind; her laugh, the way she spoke. But, now that she was in her thirties, it had faded away.

Then she ran across a picture of her grandmother in the prime of her youth. She looked so strong and vital. Tara had always been in awe of her grandmother's spirit, her ability to pull the joy out of life's most simple moments. She wondered if she would ever be able to be as resilient and strong as her grandmother had been through her whole life. She certainly didn't feel that way right now.

Just as the first tear was rolling down her cheek, she was interrupted by a knock at the door. She quickly wiped the tear away, put the pictures back in the box and stood up, walking to the front door. As she opened it, a loud creak startled her. She would need to get some WD-40 to take care of that.

"Hey, Tara. I don't know if you remember me. I'm Anita," the woman said. The attorney. The woman who had called and given her the terrible news about her grandmother. "I know this is a really challenging time for you, but I just wondered if I could chat with you a minute to talk about your grandmother's estate and some arrangements that would need to be made."

"Of course. Come on in," Tara said, stepping back and opening the door.

They walked into the living room and sat down, Anita in one of the armchairs by the fireplace and Tara on the sofa where she had been before.

"So, as you know, you are the only heir of your grandmother's estate, so you of course inherit the house and anything that was left in her bank account. Unfortunately, that wasn't a lot. Her care took a lot more money in the last few months than I think she anticipated."

Tara looked at her, confused. "What exactly happened to my grandmother? She always sounded fine on the phone. She always looked great on video. I mean, I know she was older, but I never knew anything was wrong with her health other than a bit of arthritis."

Anita smiled slightly. "She didn't want you to know. She knew that you were busy with work, and she didn't want to worry you, but your grandmother had pancreatic cancer."

Tara felt like her heart was going to stop. "Pancreatic cancer?" How in the world could she have pretended that everything was okay up until a week ago? It just didn't make any sense. "I don't understand. We would video chat most Sundays, or at least talk on the phone. Now that I think about it, maybe I didn't see her on video for the last two or three weeks, but it was just because I was working on a big story, which turned out to be a really big waste of time."

"She really tried her best to hide it. We had several conversations. I did encourage her to talk to you about what was going on so that you could come and say a proper goodbye, but she just wouldn't hear of it."

Tara didn't know whether to be sad or mad. Her grandmother was trying to protect her, but she robbed her of being able to say goodbye to the woman who had been her mother for her entire life.

"I just can't believe she didn't tell me anything.

That must've been so terrible for her to go through alone."

"She wasn't alone, if that makes you feel any better."

"What do you mean?"

"She had help from the community."

"Help from the community?" Tara wasn't surprised that people had come around to assist her grandmother in her time of need. After all, she'd lived there for so long. But why didn't any of them tell her? Why didn't any of them call and urge her to come home?

"Was she alone? In the end, I mean?" Tara asked, not sure if she wanted to know the answer to that question.

"No. From what I understand, she had friends here. And a nurse. That's where a lot of her money went at the end of her life. She had in-home health-care, so she died right there in her bedroom, surrounded by those who loved her."

For some reason, that made Tara feel better, that her grandmother had been surrounded by her favorite things and hopefully some of her favorite people. But she wanted to be there. She would've wanted to hold her grandmother's hand in those last moments to whisper the "I love you" that would have to last the rest of her lifetime. She didn't get that, and she would never understand why, but her grandmother got to make the ultimate decision. And in her last motherly act, she had tried to protect Tara from that moment of sorrow. Or maybe she was protecting herself, too.

"If it makes you feel any better, your grandmother didn't think the cancer was going to take her life. She argued with the doctors. She never believed it. She even did some trial medications and treatments for the first few weeks after she found out."

"Well, apparently none of those worked," Tara said, stating the obvious.

"No, they didn't, but she really didn't think that this cancer was going to get her. You know how stubborn she was."

Tara smiled slightly. "I do. She was one of the strongest but most stubborn women I've ever known in my life."

"Well, that stubbornness held her in good stead. She lived a full two months longer than the doctor said she would. And in the end, she just went to sleep. She wasn't feeling well that morning. A couple of people came by to check on her, make sure she was taking her medicine, eating, that sort of thing. Then the nurse showed up and said that she was showing some signs of going downhill quickly, so her friends were able to stay."

"Do you know who these friends were? I would like to thank them properly."

"I don't exactly," Anita said, acting very uncomfortable. Tara didn't understand why it would be such a big deal for her to name the people that were with her grandmother at the end. "Listen, I do want to ask you if you have any idea what your plans are for the house?"

"The house? I haven't really had a chance to think about it. I just got here."

"I understand. I'm sure you're exhausted from traveling and just the stress of losing a loved one, but I just wanted to ask in case you needed a referral to a good real estate agent or anything."

"Oh, no. Not right now. I mean, the house is paid off, so it's really not any big hurry." Normally, she would have to plan a memorial service, but her grandmother had told her many times over the years that she wanted to be cremated and didn't want money wasted on a service. Still, Tara planned - at some point when she was ready - to stand at the ocean and spread some of her grandmother's ashes.

"You're right. Well, if you need any help with

that, just let me know. Well, I had better get going. I have an appointment back at the office."

They both stood up and walked to the front door.

"Thank you for coming and for sharing what you know about my grandmother's last days. This has been really hard, even though I knew it would happen at some point."

"It's never easy to say goodbye to those we love," Anita said, reaching out and putting her hand on Tara's shoulder. "Oh, I almost forgot. Your grandmother also had a safe deposit box over at the bank. She wanted me to give you this key."

Anita retrieved the key from her pocket and handed it to Tara.

"Do you have any idea what's in it?" Tara asked.

"No, I don't. I wouldn't expect a lot of money or anything of real value, to be honest. Like I said, your grandmother's healthcare took a lot of money in those last weeks."

"I don't care about stuff like that," Tara said, shaking her head, her eyes watering. "I would give it all up just to have another day with her."

CHAPTER 3

*C*olleen had always found that getting a jolt of sugar helped her get more energy. Sure, it wasn't healthy energy, but at least it was something. Deacon had not slept well at all last night, and that left her dead on her feet today. She stopped by her grandmother's bakery. She knew pound cake was filled with sugar and would certainly give her a boost to get through the day. After all, she needed to go into the office, update some files, make a few phone calls, and then get to her pediatrician appointment to make sure Deacon was hitting all of his first milestones. There was so much to do every day. Now that she had a baby, everything seemed to take twice as long and three times as much energy.

"Well, there's my granddaughter and great-grandson," her grandmother, SuAnn, said as she walked into the bakery. Her grandmother had more energy than anybody she knew. Well, maybe except for Dixie. Dixie beat all of them.

"Hey, how's it going today?"

"Not super busy, but I expect it to pick up after lunchtime. Let me get that baby in my arms," she said, reaching out and taking Deacon from the stroller. Colleen sat down and sighed. Her grandmother eyed her carefully. "You okay?"

"Yeah. Just a little tired is all."

"Well, that's to be expected as a new mother. Babies take a lot of energy and work."

Colleen laughed under her breath. "Yeah, I don't think I really understood that until I actually had a baby."

"Is he not sleeping well?"

"Not great."

"I remember when your mother was a baby, she would squall all night long. I swear, I thought I'd never get any sleep."

"What did you do?"

"Well, you just get through it. That's what motherhood is, just getting through everything and taking good care of your children. It isn't always pretty. You don't always do it perfectly, but as long as you do it with love, that's about all anybody could ask for.

This too shall pass."

Colleen appreciated her grandmother's sage advice, but right now she needed something more concrete, something more practical. She knew she should ask her family for help. Ask Tucker for more help. Do something. But, instead she wanted to do it herself. She wanted to prove to herself that she could be a good mother, that she didn't need everybody else's help to raise her child. Maybe it was her stubborn streak. Maybe she was just too embarrassed to ask. But it was getting to where she was going to fall asleep while she walked down the sidewalk.

"Listen, if you want to go take a little time to yourself, I can keep the baby," SuAnn offered.

"No, but I appreciate it. You're trying to work."

"Well, there's nobody in here, and I can hold the baby in one arm and run the register with my other."

"No, thank you. I do appreciate the offer. I've got to get used to this."

SuAnn walked over and sat down across from her granddaughter. She reached over and put her hand on Colleen's. "Honey, you have to ask for help. Everybody can tell that you're exhausted."

"I think that's just to be expected," Colleen said.

"It is to a point, but when you need help, it's not

weakness to ask for it. You have a community of people around you, and we're all here for you."

"I know, and I appreciate it. I really do, but I don't want to impose on anybody. I should be able to do this. This is what moms do."

"Yes, but you're a *new* mom. You're still learning, and your body's exhausted from having a baby. You know, growing a person takes a lot of energy out of you."

Colleen nodded. "I suppose so."

"Well, the offer stands. Any time you need to bring this little guy to me, I am happy to keep him. You know, I might be older, but I'm still capable."

"I know, Grandma. I would never think otherwise," Colleen said forcing a smile.

"Now, what do you say to a big slab of peach pound cake and a nice cup of coffee?"

Colleen nodded her head. "Yes. I think I definitely need the sugar rush."

The next day, Tara decided that the first thing she needed to do was go to the grocery store and fill the house with food so she didn't starve to death. She wasn't sure how long she was going to be in Seagrove, and she still had to work up the courage to go open the safe deposit box her grandmother had left for her. It wasn't like she had to go anywhere quickly. She had no job. She had no relationship. It was just her floating around in the world all by herself.

As she walked down the sidewalk in Seagrove, she looked at all the different shops and places she wanted to make time to visit. The bookstore, the bakery, the coffee shop. There were lots of places to go, and then there was the beach. She hadn't been to the beach in a long time. Sure, she drove past it when she was on her visits to see her grandmother, but she hadn't walked on the beach in many years. It had been her most favorite thing to do as a kid and even through high school, but it held a lot of memories that she wasn't sure she could take right now.

As she rounded the corner with two grocery bags in her arms, she ran right into somebody. She almost knocked her own self to the ground. As she pulled the grocery bags down slightly so she could look to see who it was, she was shocked to see her childhood best friend, Noah, standing there on the sidewalk looking just as surprised as she did. He was older now, but still just as handsome as he had always been. Tall, broad-shouldered, crystal clear blue eyes like the ocean not far away. He'd been handsome back then, but he was downright gorgeous now.

They both stared at each other for a long moment, as if each of them thought they might be in a dream. Finally, Noah smiled slightly, looking down at her. "Tara? Is that you?"

She returned his smile. "It's me. I can't believe I actually ran into you, like literally."

He laughed. She remembered that laugh well. They had giggled their entire childhood as they collected sea glass on the beach. That was one of their favorite pastimes. All the memories of growing up with him as her best friend flooded into her mind. There wasn't a bad one among the bunch. Over the years, they had just drifted apart with life handing them all kinds of different scenarios that would pull them further and further away from each other. Maybe she should have made more of an effort to stay in touch. After all, she was sure he was on social media somewhere. But college and then work had taken her focus, and Noah had fallen into the history of her life.

"Wow. It's been a long time since I've seen you." For some reason, Tara glanced down at his left hand searching for a wedding ring. There was none. Not that it mattered. She had never dated Noah, although she'd had a big crush on him during high school that he never knew about. All the girls had a crush on Noah, and that was a big part of the problem. Tara found herself getting very jealous that her best friend was getting so much attention.

"You probably heard that my grandmother passed away. I'm here to settle her estate and figure out what to do with the house."

He leaned in and took both of the grocery bags out of her arms. Just one of the southern gentleman type things Noah would always do. "I know, and I'm so sorry. I know how much you loved her and how much she loved you."

"So, now I have to decide exactly what I'm going to do, and I'm sort of in a part of my life that is a little up in the air." Why was she telling him this?

He cocked his head slightly. "Anything you want to talk about?"

She paused for a moment and then shook her head. "Not really. What are you doing these days? Wife and kids?"

He laughed. "Divorced three years ago."

"Oh, sorry to hear that."

"It just wasn't the right person. You know how it is."

She wondered if he had somehow heard about the breakup with her fiancé. That would be pretty impossible, but it did go through her mind. "Yeah, I get it. Where are you working these days?" Tara hated small talk.

"I actually have my own shop right there on the square."

"Really?" She leaned sideways and looked around the square. "Which one?"

"Right over there next to the coffee shop. I sell sea glass art."

Tara's heart felt like it stopped in her chest for a moment. Sea glass, the one thing that they had done together their whole lives.

She had never expected that that would be what he was doing now. "You make art with sea glass?" she said, sounding very dense.

"I do. I opened the place a couple of years ago. Sort of a way to get over my divorce and to stop feeling like a giant failure."

She laughed under her breath. "I totally understand that. What were you doing before that?"

"I was working as a high school art teacher. Sometimes I still fill in over at the local high school."

She smiled. "I can see that. A big kid at heart. I bet the students love you."

He shrugged his shoulders. "Sometimes. Listen, can I carry these back to the house for you?"

She shook her head. "No, thank you. I'm not that far, and I need the exercise."

He looked her up and down quickly. "You look fine to me." For some reason, Tara got a shiver up her spine. This was Noah. She couldn't look at him like that. He was her best friend from all those years ago, not somebody she would ever want to get romantically involved with. At least that's what she was telling herself as the chill continued running up her back. "I would love to get together sometime while you're here. Maybe have a cup of coffee or lunch?"

She nodded quickly. "Of course. We really need to catch up." Even though they were having a nice conversation, things felt awkward to Tara. Conversation didn't flow like it used to all those years ago. They were like two acquaintances just running into each other, but she still would like to get together with him and catch up. There were lots of stories they could share from when they grew up. Things that happened in school. Gossip about other people.

"Hand me your phone," he said. Without asking any questions, Tara pulled it out of her pocket and handed it over as he slid the grocery bags back into her arms. "I'm going to put my phone number in here. When you're ready to get together, just send me a text or call me." He reached over and slid the phone back in her pocket. "It was good to see you, Tara."

"It was great to see you, too."

As he walked down the sidewalk without turning around, she looked back at him. He still walked the same. He still sounded the same. But, she had to wonder if they got together for coffee, was it going to feel as awkward as this interaction had felt? She hoped not because she really needed somebody right now, and maybe Noah was the right person to lean on.

Julie had taken a much needed day off of work and spent the whole time on her computer. As she typed away, she continued to check her email every few minutes. Even though the notification sound was on, she still couldn't help but go over and make sure that she hadn't gotten any messages. This is what her life had been like for the last several months. She had never been somebody who gave into stress and anxiety. She always found a way out of it, but lately she was stuck in it. It was like those scary movies from her childhood where people got stuck in quicksand. She worried so much about quicksand as a kid, she honestly thought that when she grew up, it was going to be a common day-to-day problem.

She hadn't ever seen any quicksand in her life, but that didn't mean that she didn't feel like she was stuck in it. She checked her email again and noticed a new message had just come in. She had caught it before the dinging. She closed her eyes and sucked in a deep breath, blowing it out slowly through her mouth like her sister Janine had taught her in yoga class.

As she clicked the email, she was crestfallen yet again. Why was there never any good news? She closed her laptop and put her head on top of it. Maybe she should get out of the house and go do something, take a walk on the beach, go shopping, buy a plane ticket and leave town. She wasn't sure which one was the best option. She knew Dawson was worried about her. He had mentioned it a few times, but she didn't want to worry him. She didn't want to put her problem on him when he was so busy with everything else. Helping to run the inn, doing his contracting work, building furniture. Dawson kept busy.

She was trying to do the same, but her mind was always rattled. She was always distracted. She decided to get up and make herself another cup of coffee. She had already had three this morning and could feel her hands shaking a bit, but she needed to stay as energized and awake today as possible. She had a lot of work to do on the computer. She wasn't feeling super motivated, of course, but the coffee would keep her going long enough to get her work done.

Thankfully, Meg was running the bookstore today. They were only open for half the day since it was Sunday, so it was a good day for her to be off. She knew she should be sitting outside in the sunshine, enjoying the sound of the ocean waves lapping at the shore instead of sitting in her office, staring out the window, wishing that she was anywhere else. This whole thing wasn't what she thought it was going to be. This project that she had been working on secretly for so long was falling to pieces, and she had no one to talk to about it. Sometimes she thought about getting a therapist, which was ridiculous because she could just talk to her friends and family. All of them would be willing to support her and help her through it, but for some reason she just couldn't bring herself to do it. Just as she was getting up to walk into the kitchen for that fourth cup of coffee, she heard a knock at the front door. She walked over and opened it to see Dixie standing there.

She smiled broadly and handed her a small white box. "Brought you some blueberry muffins. These are the kind my mama used to make. I think you should sell them at the bookstore."

Julie smiled, "So are you offering to make regular blueberry muffins and bring them to the bookstore for me to sell?"

Dixie shook her head. "No, I don't think I am offering that. I was going to give you the recipe."

She laughed. "I think I have enough on my plate. Come on in." She stepped back and opened the door. Dixie walked inside and into the living room.

"What are you doing today? Meg said you were off when I went by there."

"Oh, just taking some much needed time."

"By sitting in the house by yourself? You don't even have any lights on in here, Julie."

Julie walked over and put the box on the coffee table and sat down on the sofa. Dixie sat across from her in one of the armchairs by the window. They were designed using embroidery made by Dawson's grandmother all those years ago.

"I was actually upstairs working in my office."

"Honey, it's a beautiful day outside, and you live right on the ocean. Why don't you go out there and eat some lunch or take a walk?"

Julie chuckled. "Did you come over here to tell me what to do?"

"Well, it seems like somebody needs to."

"What is that supposed to mean?"

Dixie sighed. "Listen, I've been asking you for weeks now what's going on. I know something's wrong. Dawson is worried."

"He told you that?"

"He did."

"Well, there's nothing to be worried about," Julie said not making eye contact.

Dixie slapped her knees. "Listen, I'm not leaving this house until you tell me the truth."

"I already told you the truth," Julie said, lying completely.

"No, you didn't. I'm a good judge of character, and I know you like I know the back of my hand. There is no way things are okay, and I'm just not going to leave here until you tell me the truth."

Julie laughed and leaned back against the sofa. "Well, then, I guess you live here now."

Dixie crossed her arms and leaned back against the chair. "Well, I guess I do."

"Why are you being like this?"

"You said that if anything was wrong, you would talk to me about it, and you lied," Dixie said.

Julie's eyes just about bugged out of her head. "Excuse me?"

"Honey, I know something's wrong. You're not acting like yourself, and I would be a terrible friend if I didn't push you to tell me what's going on so I can help you."

Julie sat silently for a moment and leaned her head back, closing her eyes.

"You can't help me. Nobody can."

Dixie stood up and walked over to the sofa, sitting down next to her. "Okay, now you're really worrying me. Tell me the truth, Julie. What is going on?" She reached over and took Julie's hand in hers. It felt good to feel someone holding her hand.

"It has been a rough morning. Actually, it has been a rough few weeks. I don't want to burden anybody else, and really, it's a silly problem. It's not something that should even be a problem."

"Tell me," Dixie said firmly.

Julie threw her other hand up in the air. "Okay,

fine. You know I've always wanted to write a book right?"

"Of course. You've said that many times."

"Well, I've been working on a novel for the last year."

"Really? That's incredible, Julie!"

"Well, I thought so too until I started sending out query letters."

"You mean to agents?"

"Yes, and publishers, of course."

"So, I take that to mean that you're not getting positive responses?"

"No, I'm not. Every single one of them has said they're not interested. Most of them don't give me any real feedback, but all I know is that they all think I stink."

Dixie patted her on the leg. "Do you know how many authors get rejected dozens of times before they publish a book?"

Julie stood up and crossed her arms pacing in front of the fireplace. "Well, maybe they're stronger than me because I can't handle this. I've gotten so many rejections. I mean, nobody even wants to represent me as my agent. What does that say?"

"That they're idiots," Dixie said, standing up and walking closer. "There are stories of so many artistic people, whether it's a singer or an author, who got rejected a million times and then became big celebrities."

"I don't think I'm going to become a celebrity," Julie said, rolling her eyes.

"Well, maybe not. Not everybody aspires to that."

"The only thing I wanted was to see my book in the bookstore. To be able to sit at a table and sign them for people. To be able to see my book cover and hold my book in my hand. I don't need to make a bunch of money. I'm comfortable. I have a great life. But, I wanted to tell a story about a woman like me."

"And you told that story. You wrote the book, right?"

"Well, yes. But, if I never get it published, it really doesn't matter, does it?"

"Honey, there's not just one way to skin a cat."

"I've always hated that saying, Dixie. You know that."

"Okay, well say whatever saying you want. I'm just telling you that there's not just one way to get your book published."

"What do you mean?"

"You know we have some self-published authors

whose books we carry at the bookstore. You love some of those books."

"Yes, that's true."

"Why can't you pursue it that way? Why can't you self-publish?"

Julie shook her head. "Oh, I wouldn't even know where to begin. I'm sure that's a very difficult process. I'm not smart enough for all of that," she said laughing under her breath. Dixie walked over and put her hands on Julie's shoulders.

"You're plenty smart enough for all that. Also, you have to tell Dawson what's going on."

"No. Absolutely not. He's so busy these days. He's got so many jobs. I'm not going to pile on something extra to worry about."

"Honey, when you're married, you share the load. That's one of the perks of being married."

"I'll tell him eventually, but promise me you won't tell him. Let me at least check into this self-publishing thing and see if I can figure it out."

"Why don't you give one of those authors a call from the store? I'm sure they'd be glad to give you the information on how they got started."

"I guess it wouldn't hurt," Julie said, starting to feel a little bit better.

"I'll just say one more thing. When these agents

and publishing companies are declining you, just remember that they're probably sitting in a cubicle somewhere looking at hundreds of books every week, and it's just their one opinion. Just one person's opinion. That doesn't mean that you're not a good writer."

"Thank you, Dixie. You've made me feel a little better."

"Well, good. Now, I'm ordering you to get out of this house. You can't sit here in the dark looking at your computer for the rest of the day. That's not good for your mental health. Make yourself a sandwich and go sit out there on that beach."

"Yes, ma'am," Julie said, laughing as she saluted Dixie. Dixie pulled her into a tight hug. She was so thankful for the motherly presence that Dixie provided. Even though her own mother lived in town and had gotten better over the years, Dixie would always stand out as somebody she respected and adored.

CHAPTER 4

Tara stood outside of Beachcombers,
Noah's sea glass art shop in downtown
Seagrove. The sign was whimsically painted with
blue and green, and it swayed from two little chains,
as the ocean breeze passed through town. She stood
there with memories of her childhood, as she looked
around at all the different shops. She remembered
sun-drenched days, laughter, ice cream cones, and
running all over town doing things with Noah. She
took in a deep breath and pushed the door open. Sea
glass made a familiar sound as a chime welcomed
her into the shop.

She could smell the scent of the ocean, probably
from a candle burning on the counter. It was a hint
of sandalwood that enveloped her as she walked
inside, taking her back to a time when her life was

carefree and innocent. The shop was beautiful, a testament to Noah's talent and their shared past of collecting sea glass. She looked around and wondered if any of the items that he'd made had sea glass from their childhood. She doubted it, of course. It had been a very long time. He had probably collected lots of sea glass between the last time she'd seen him and now.

Sunlight was streaming through the windows, casting a prism of rainbows across the room, as each glint of light danced off the sea glass art. He had a range of items, from Christmas trees made of sea glass, each with branches adorned in different colors of emerald and blue with hints of amber.

He also had wind chimes, of course, hanging from the ceiling, all unique with different colors. He even had jewelry laying across one of the countertops, necklaces and earrings mostly, with the occasional ring and bracelet. She was very impressed by the breadth and depth of what he offered. It was funny, because she had never known Noah to be an artist. When they were kids, he did sit around drawing quite a bit, but she didn't ever think that he would take their hobby of running around on the beach looking for sea glass and turn it into an actual business. She had no idea he could do these things.

It just goes to show that, sometimes, you think you know somebody, but you really don't.

Behind the counter a teenage girl with tanned skin and bleached blonde hair looked up from a book she was reading. "Hey, can I help you with anything?" she asked, her voice carrying across the shop.

"Just looking, but thank you," Tara said. "Is Noah here, by any chance?"

"Oh, he just popped out to get some more supplies at the store, but he should be back soon. You're welcome to look around in the meantime," she said, with a friendly smile. Tara had missed this, that small town charm, the place where everybody looked at you and waved, knew your name, knew your business.

She nodded and thanked the young woman before wandering through the store, her fingers trailing across the smooth and weathered edges of sea glass. He had some framed mosaics on the wall, with all different colors, made into various scenes. Beach scenes, mostly. Some of them were more intricate than others. There were some cute ones where just one or two pieces of sea glass were used and then, animals were drawn around them. One in particular was a little mouse with a top hat. Its body was a piece of blue sea glass, and it had a little green hat on its head and everything drawn around it to make a complete scene.

She walked over to the jewelry counter and picked up a particularly beautiful necklace. Five different pieces of colored sea glass hung from it in a row, each one more vibrant than the next. It glowed under the warm lights of the shop. As she started to look at a stunning piece of artwork hanging on the wall, which depicted the Seagrove coastline complete with a miniature lighthouse made with black and white glass, the door chimed. She turned and saw Noah stepping into his shop, his arms full of bags of crafting materials.

"Tara? I wasn't expecting to see you here," he said. He put the bags on the counter for the young woman to take to the back. A warm smile crossed his face with crinkles at the corners of his deep sea-blue eyes.

"I was just passing by and thought I'd come in and take a look," she said. She swore her heart skipped a beat. "Your work is incredible. I can't believe that you can do all of this. I never knew."

He blushed slightly. "Thanks. You know how I've always loved sea glass. Every time I make a piece, it brings back memories of our childhood. All those days we spent combing the beach."

She chuckled. "We did have quite the collection. Is there anything in here that was made from the sea glass we collected all those years ago?" she asked, hopefully. He shook his head.

"Nothing here. No. That was a long time ago, Tara."

"I know. I just thought maybe," she said before stopping herself.

"So what is your plan for today?"

"Well, I'm going to go get some lunch and then I thought I'd just walk around and explore a bit. Take a day off from going through my grandmother's house. It's pretty stressful."

"I imagine so."

"I thought I would go over to the bookstore, get some good books to read. My grandmother has books at the house, but nothing I would ever read."

He laughed. "Oh yeah? What did she have?"

"Mostly cookbooks and those old-time romance novels. Just not my thing."

"No romance?" he asked, his eyebrow lifting.

"Not right now." She didn't want to elaborate on what had gone on in her life recently.

"I was hoping you would give me a call after

running into you the other day, but since you're here right now, how about I take you to lunch? Welcome you back to town?"

"I don't know..." Tara hesitated, a whirlwind of emotion swirling inside of her stomach. As much as she would love the comfort of Noah's presence, she didn't want to give him the wrong idea. She wasn't staying in Seagrove, but it would be good to catch up. And how did she know he had any interest in her, anyway? After all, they were always nothing more than friends. "You know, I would like that. Let's have lunch," she said smiling.

"Great. Let me just do a couple of things in the back, and then, we can head out."

Colleen sat with her sister Meg at a table outside of the cafe on the square that they loved to go to. It was a wonderful, charming spot that allowed them to experience the warmth of early summer and wave at all their friends as they walked by.

The square was always alive with a gentle hum of conversation. She could hear the laughs of people passing by and the soft rustling of the Spanish moss hanging in the trees overhead.

Each of them ordered their favorite lunch meals. Colleen got her typical chicken salad sandwich on a croissant with a side of french fries and coleslaw. Meg chose a po-boy with crispy shrimp spilling out of the toasted baguette. They both had their requisite glasses of sweet tea, little beads of condensation running down the sides of the clear glasses in the warm sun as they sat waiting for their food.

Colleen looked at her little sister who had become an expert at being a mother. Her lively little daughter, Vivi, was happily drawing on a piece of paper in her coloring book as she sat beside them. Meg had ordered her a grilled cheese sandwich, which was her favorite. She saw Vivi eat grilled cheese sandwiches more than just about anything else.

She continued drawing with her crayons, seeming to create a beach scene on her piece of paper. Colleen felt a pang of envy in her heart. She admired her sister, who had become a mother at a very young age, but she had handled motherhood with such strength and grace. And now Colleen found herself struggling. Her baby was just a few weeks old, and despite being the older sister,

Colleen felt like she was already failing in her new role as a mother.

She wanted to ask for help. Every day it got harder. She wanted to ask for advice, but her pride and the fear of being embarrassed in front of her family and friends held her back.

When their meals arrived, they ate as they chatted away about this and that. Colleen struggled to keep her eyes open. She was always tired these days. Thankfully, the chicken salad sandwich was the perfect blend of crunchy and creamy today, and the sweet tea was a soothing balm against the growing heat of the day. Summers in the South Carolina Lowcountry were hot. There was no doubt about that. It wasn't quite there yet, but it was getting close.

"Meg, have you noticed anything different about Mom lately?" Colleen asked, trying to change her thoughts from worrying about herself to worrying about someone else.

Meg looked up. "I have. She seems a little distant. I can't quite put my finger on what it is. It's like she's got something going on that she's not telling anybody about."

Colleen nodded. "That's what I've seen also, and

it's not like her to keep things from us. She's always been the rock of the family."

Meg nodded. "That's true, but I know that she wouldn't want to worry us with anything. Hopefully, it's nothing major. Do you think it is?"

Colleen shrugged her shoulders. "I don't know. I would like to think she would confide in us if there was something really awful going on. Do you think she's having marriage trouble with Dawson?"

Meg laughed. "Absolutely not. Working at the bookstore now, I get to see them more often, and I swear they're like a couple of school kids. It's kind of gross."

Colleen laughed. "Yeah, I've seen that before. Do you think maybe Dad has been getting in touch with her? Upsetting her somehow?"

"I wouldn't think so. He knows not to mess with Mom. Dawson would find him and do some damage, I think. I barely hear from him."

"Same here. I think the last thing I got was an email. Well, whatever it is, I think we need to try to figure it out. We're a family, after all. We need to be there for each other," Meg said, eyeing her sister carefully.

"Don't look at me like that," Colleen said, taking another bite of her sandwich. "I told you, I'm fine."

"You know, the women in this family can be very frustrating," Meg said, rolling her eyes as she reached over and pinched Vivi's cheek. "Can you believe this one is going to be going to kindergarten soon?"

Colleen smiled over at her niece. "Are you excited, Vivi?"

Vivi threw her hands in the air. "I don't know," she said. Vivi was always a kid who sort of flew by the seat of her pants. She didn't seem to let much bother her. "I heard we get chocolate milk there, so I like that." Colleen chuckled.

"Such a simple little life you have going, Vivi."

After a pause for a few moments, Meg spoke again. "We should do something for Mom. Maybe we could have a family dinner at my place, but just the women and kids. She might open up if it's just us."

Colleen nodded her head, popping the last bite of her sandwich into her mouth. "That sounds good. I can bring dessert."

"Okay. I'll let you know what day and time," Meg said, wiping her mouth and then taking another sip of sweet tea.

Colleen watched Meg as she interacted with Vivi, reprimanding her a bit for getting crayon marks on her brand new shirt. She hoped that she could rise to the occasion and be as good of a mother as her own mother had been to her, and as Meg was to Vivi.

Tara and Noah sat on a rustic wooden bench just outside of the food truck near the water. It was nestled against the beautiful backdrop of Seagrove's marshland. The vibrant yellow truck, which was painted with pictures of corn and shrimp, was a local favorite, according to Noah. It was known for its authentic Lowcountry cuisine, which was something both of them loved. The smell of seafood and spices blew through the air, mingling with the salty breeze from the ocean and the organic smell of the marsh. They had both chosen to have shrimp and grits, as well as a side of homemade hush puppies. Tara had never tasted something as good in her life. Although she'd loved living in the city for a long time, she could never get authentic Lowcountry food there, and right now, she was so happy to be sitting in her favorite place on earth.

As they shared a basket of hush puppies, with their crunchy exteriors giving way to a soft, fluffy inside, she felt like she had transported herself back in time. The surrounding scenery seemed to come alive. The marsh was full of all different kinds of animals and insects, along with rotting organic matter beneath. It had a certain smell, the pluff mud sending its scent out into the air as the water lapped gently at the shore. She could hear seagulls soaring overhead, calling out a familiar tune that was always connected to coastal life.

Their conversation was full of memories each one of them shared. It was something special for Tara. It had been so long since she had talked to someone, other than her grandmother, who knew her history, her previous life, who knew who she really was. Right now, she felt adrift, like she had no future. Her career had been so important to her, and now it was seemingly gone. She didn't know if she would ever work as a journalist again. How embarrassing. How discouraging. And it was her own fault. She hadn't been as careful as she always had. She had let her emotions and her personal problems cloud her judgment, and now she felt like her life was over.

Noah interrupted her very negative thought process as he brought up a middle school science fair project they had done together. It was about sea glass, of course, and they were trying to demonstrate the ocean's currents.

"You were so determined to find every color of sea glass imaginable," he said, laughing. "I swear we must have walked ten miles that day, up and down the beach."

She smiled at the memory.

"And then there was that time that we snuck into the old lighthouse on a dare. Do you remember that? I was so scared we were going to get caught and my grandmother was going to kill me, but you just wanted to see the view from the top."

He nodded. "Yes, I remember. We were definitely not old enough to climb up the lighthouse, but that view was worth it. Remember how we could see the entire town square from up there?"

Then their conversation shifted to their high school years, filled with memories of football games, bonfires on the beach, and seemingly endless summer days. Tara remembered her junior prom and how they had gone as friends. The whole time, she was desperately in love with him, but never told him. She couldn't believe she had kept that secret all these years.

"You stepped on my toes during every dance," she

said, teasing him. "But it was still one of the best nights I've ever had."

He chuckled under his breath. "I was a terrible dancer. You were very patient with me. But remember, when we got in that sudden rainstorm on the way home from the beach? We were soaked down to the bone, but we couldn't stop laughing."

"Yes, and we just danced in the rain like nobody was watching," she said. "It felt like we were living something out of a movie.

She remembered how that night she had hoped that he would suddenly profess his love to her and kiss her right there in the rain, but it didn't happen.

They also talked about a senior year project they had where they had to team up to create a photo-journalism piece about life in Seagrove.

"You were always behind the camera, capturing moments that most of us would overlook," Noah said. "You always just had this way of seeing things in a different way."

She remembered how they had spent so many afternoons wandering around to all the shops, her taking pictures, and him sitting down to draw different things that he saw.

"You were just my unofficial assistant," she said. "I couldn't have done anything without your eye for detail. You always found the best sea glass and then left it sitting there so I could find it later. I wasn't as good at looking for it like you were."

They continued reminiscing for quite some time, when Noah looked down at his watch.

"Well, I hate to cut our lunch short, but I should probably get back and relieve Tiffany," he said, referring to the young woman that was running the register when she got there. "This has been a lot of fun. I'm really glad we got to do this."

They stood up and threw their trash in a nearby can before starting the walk back to the town square.

"I hope we get to do this again. How long are you planning to stay in Seagrove?"

She shrugged her shoulders. "I'm not sure. It could be a few days. It could be forever. Right now, things are kind of up in the air."

"Anything you want to talk about?" he asked as they made their way up the path to the road.

"Not right now," she said. "I'd rather just linger here in the memories."

CHAPTER 5

*D*awson found Julie sitting alone on the beach, her figure silhouetted against the fading light of the late afternoon sun. He could see the big, beautiful ocean stretched out in front of her, a seemingly endless canvas of blues and greens. The waves were gently lapping at the shore, and her toes were just barely touching them. He approached her quietly, the soft crunch of the sand under his shoes breaking the silence. As he got closer, he could see that she was staring at the horizon, lost in thought. She had been this way a lot lately, and he was worried about her. She was normally so positive and confident, but she seemed weighed down by something. And no matter how many times he asked, she just wouldn't share it with him. The more he asked about it, the more she seemed to quietly retreat into herself.

"Hey. Everything okay?" he said, not wanting to startle her. He sat down next to her.

She turned and smiled at him. "Yeah, I just didn't hear you. I'm fine. Just enjoying some quiet time on the beach. We're so lucky that we get to live here."

He wasn't convinced. He knew her so well, and he sensed that something was off. The way that she wouldn't quite look into his eyes, the slight strain in her voice. These were signs that she was saying one thing and feeling another.

"You know you can talk to me about anything, right?" he said, putting his arm around her. "If something's bothering you, I'm here."

She sighed and put her head on his shoulder. "I appreciate it, really. But I'm okay. I've just been a little tired lately. That's all." Her tone was dismissive, but he could tell that something else was going on.

"Have you thought about seeing the doctor? Maybe you need some blood work."

"I'm fine, honey. Really," she said, looking up at him. The dying light was casting shadows across her face, highlighting the tiredness in her eyes. He wanted to push harder, but he knew she would just retreat further. Julie was a strong and independent woman, and he knew that she would come to him when she was ready to talk.

"Okay," he said, finally relenting. "But you remember that I am here for you. We're a partnership. You don't ever have to go through anything alone. I will stand with you always."

Her eyes looked like they were starting to water, but then she blinked back any tears that threatened to fall. She nodded silently and then turned and looked back at the ocean. They sat there for a while longer, side by side, his arm around her shoulders as the sun dipped lower in the sky, leaving behind it hues of orange and pink. The sound of the waves were a comforting rhythm as always, a reminder of the constant ebb and flow that was life. But still, Dawson was concerned. He couldn't shake the feeling that his wife was carrying a burden that was too heavy for her, and he wanted to take it from her more than anything.

Mornings were Tara's favorite. She loved how every day was a fresh, new beginning, and this morning was no different. She had things to do around the house. She needed to finally get over to the bank and open the safe deposit box. She wasn't sure if today was that day yet or not.

As she walked from the bedroom to the kitchen, she could see the morning sun out over the marsh just beginning to peek over the horizon. As she turned the corner to go into the kitchen to make herself a pot of coffee, she heard a light tapping at the front door. She was wrapped in a cozy white robe with her hair tousled from sleep. She padded softly over to the door, slightly irritated that someone was there so early. She couldn't imagine who it was.

Opening the door, she was greeted by the sight of Noah, who was standing there with a hopeful smile on his face. He was dressed in casual beach clothing, a lightweight hoodie and shorts. His eyes were bright with enthusiasm. She recognized that look.

"Good morning, Tara," he said cheerfully.

There was only one other person on earth who was more of a morning person than Tara, and it was Noah.

"I know it's early, but I thought maybe we could go out and search for some sea glass on the beach. You know, like old times. The tide is low. It's the perfect time for us to go out and do it."

Still groggy from sleep, Tara hesitated. "Noah, I

don't know. It's really early. I was planning to kind of start my day off slowly," she said, trying to stifle a yawn.

Noah was undeterred. "I know, I know. But trust me, it's worth it. You know the beach is beautiful at this hour. We'll have it all to ourselves, and it's the very best time to find sea glass. It's been so long since I've been out searching. A lot of my art pieces are made with sea glass that are shipped in from somewhere else. But don't you remember how we used to race to see who could find the best pieces?"

His words sent a flicker of nostalgia through Tara's heart. She had so many memories of cool early summer mornings spent combing that beach. All they could hear over the waves was their own laughter. She couldn't deny the fact that she really would love to revisit those carefree days of child-hood, even if it was just for one morning.

"I'm not sure I want to do that this morning..." she started.

Seeing her hesitation, Noah spoke up again. "Come on. It's going to be like an adventure. I'll even buy you breakfast after. How about that?"

The promise of a good breakfast and the chance to relive a part of her childhood swayed Tara. The

warmth of the memories and Noah's absolute enthusiasm broke through.

"Okay, fine. You win," she conceded. "Let me just
go get dressed and make some coffee real quick. Give
me a few minutes."

His face lit up with a grin. "I'll wait for you
outside."

She closed the door and couldn't help but feel a
sense of excitement bubbling up inside of her. She
quickly ran upstairs and dressed in some comfortable clothing suitable for a morning on the beach.
She put on her sneakers and laced them up, started
the coffeepot, and then poured it into a travel mug.

When she stepped outside, she felt the
refreshing chill of the early summer air, a promise of
a new day. They set off together toward the beach
like they had done a million times as kids, the sky
above them painted in beautiful hues of pink and
orange. It was a day of possibilities.

Colleen was dead on her feet again this
morning. The baby had kept her and Tucker
up all night. She felt terrible for Tucker because he
had to go out of town on a business trip for a couple

of days. He was going to Atlanta for a toy convention. He just couldn't miss it. It was too important for their business. In an effort to get herself to wake up, she drank several cups of coffee and put Deacon into the stroller so they could walk around the square. She meandered through the newly sunlit streets of Seagrove, trying to will herself to get more energy.

It was a serene morning, beautiful skies, perfect temperature, but her mind was clouded with the fatigue that often comes with new motherhood. Although she felt overwhelmed, she was still reluctant to share her struggles with others, believing that she should be able to handle this on her own. That it would eventually pass. That it was normal. As she rounded the corner near the bookstore, she almost collided with her Aunt Janine, who was balancing her own kid on her hip.

"Hey, it's good to see you and little Deacon," she said, leaning over and touching his cheek. He smiled, which was something he had just started doing recently. "How have you been adjusting to new motherhood?"

Colleen managed a weary smile. "As you know, it's been a journey for sure. Deacon is a perfect baby. Well, most of the time. Not last night," she said, laughing.

Janine nodded sympathetically, shifting Madison onto her other hip. "I completely get it. You know, when we adopted Madison, it turned our world upside down. Here I am, in my late forties, and I was adopting a child. It was a lot for us to handle. It was a lot to get accustomed to."

They stood there chatting for a few moments, with Janine sharing some of her own advice about being a new mother. Colleen finally admitted to her that she had a lot of sleepless nights, and with Tucker working so much lately, she felt like she wasn't getting good rest. It was comforting to talk to somebody who actually understood.

"Not to change the subject," Janine said, "but how's your mom doing? I haven't gotten to catch up with her lately, but the last time I saw her, she seemed to be a little preoccupied with something."

"You know, Meg and I were talking about that. She's been a little distant lately, but she insists that she's okay. We thought maybe we might have a girl's dinner one night with just us and the kids. I was going to reach out to you."

"That sounds like a good idea. You know, we all need to surround each other with support. We're a family and a community. She's probably just going through something and doesn't want to talk about it, but we have to keep an eye on her even if she says she's fine. That's typically what she does. Julie never wants anybody to see her cracks." Madison began to fuss a little on Janine's hip. "You know, if you ever need a break or anything or just somebody to talk to, I'm here. I know how isolating the first few months of being a mother can feel."

"Thank you. That means a lot. Maybe we can even have a play date sometime. Although, Deacon isn't exactly an exciting friend just yet," she said, smiling.

"I'd love that. We can get some coffee and just hang out one day. For now, I'd better get to the yoga studio. I have an early class that I need to teach."

As they parted ways, Colleen felt a renewed sense of camaraderie and hope. Her aunt understood. Her sister understood. Most women who'd had children would understand her plight, but for some reason, she'd had such a hard time sharing it. Maybe that was the secret. Not carrying everything alone but sharing it with others who understood. Maybe that was the biggest act of strength and self-care she could give herself.

T he morning air was crisp and invigorating as Noah and Tara made their way to that familiar stretch of beach where they had spent so many hours as children. As the sun was continuing to climb in the sky, getting ready for a hot early summer day in the Lowcountry, a golden hue was cast over the ocean. It turned the water into a sparkling expanse that stretched beyond the horizon to places unseen.

Tara felt a mixture of emotions swirling around in her. Certainly, she had nostalgia for the beach and for the activity of looking for sea glass with Noah. It was soothing to be around the waves that were coming in and out like clockwork. She could taste the salty tang of the sea air on her lips, which was also comforting, but it brought her back to simpler times. Picnics on the beach with her grandmother. Sunday afternoon strolls on the sand. Aside from sea glass hunting with Noah, she had so many wonderful memories of her grandmother. She was blessed to have been raised in a place like this, so wild and yet so tame at the same time.

Those times were a far cry from the complexities that she now faced in her life. It felt weird to have Noah walking beside her again, carrying a bucket to collect sea glass just like he did when they were kids. He seemed at ease, comfortable, but Tara noticed a subtle tension in his shoulders. Maybe there were unspoken words. Maybe there were resentful thoughts bubbling under the surface.

They reached a particularly pebbled section of the beach and began their search, each of them scanning the sand for glints of sea glass. It was a familiar activity, one that had not required any words to be exchanged between them. They knew what to do. Each of them got whisked away in the sense of joy and discovery. It felt like it was more than just a normal hunt for ocean treasures.

After a few minutes of silence that was becoming more and more awkward, Tara felt an unexpected compulsion to tell some of her secrets to unburden herself.

"I never thought that I'd be back here. Not like this," she said. "I lost my job. And my fiancé and I... well, we broke up. So basically the entire life I had built the last many years just exploded all at once."

Noah paused in his search and turned to face her. His expression was one of genuine concern. "I'm so sorry, Tara. I had no idea. What happened?"

She sighed. "I made a big mistake at work, like a really big one. I didn't check my sources closely enough, and it blew up into a huge ordeal. Lost my job over it. Probably lost my career, if I'm being honest. I was very distracted because John and I had recently broken up and it was painful. Looking back, I know he wasn't the right one for me but I wasted two years of my life. Now I just feel very adrift, like I've lost my direction."

"And then you lost your grandmother," Noah said.

"Yes. And trust me, that makes everything immensely worse. She was always the person that I could talk to about anything. She gave the greatest advice, and now she's not here. In a way, I'm happy she's not here because I wouldn't want her to see me as such a failure."

He dropped the bucket and put his hands on her shoulders. "Are you kidding me? You're not a failure. You're one of the most successful people I know."

"Then you should raise your standards," she said, laughing under her breath.

"Tara, you chased your dreams. You left Seagrove even though you loved it and your grandmother."

"And now I'm right back here."

"Well, to be fair, you would have had to come back here anyway to settle your grandmother's estate."

"I know, but I have nowhere to go now. I still have my place back in Atlanta, of course, but I am in no hurry to get back there and show my face. I haven't even heard from any of my friends at the TV station. I'm sure everybody is annoyed with me. I'll be surprised if there's not some sort of legal trouble I get into for that story."

"You can't think about all the what-ifs, Tara. You have to be in the here and now. The only moment we have is the present. And I can't imagine how hard all of that must be on you, but I know without a shadow of a doubt that you'll find your way again."

They paused for a moment, the only noise the sound of the ocean waves coming in and out.

"Thank you," was all Tara could manage to say.

"I'm sorry I haven't been there for you over the years, Tara. When you left for college, I guess I felt abandoned. I know it was selfish, but I held onto that grudge for a long time. Eventually, I left Seagrove for a while. I've only been back for the last couple of years."

She looked at him, surprise etched on her face. "I had no idea that you felt abandoned, Noah. I was so caught up in my own stuff. I just didn't realize that I was actually leaving you behind. I'm sorry, truly."

His face softened, and he offered a small, sincere

smile. "I guess we both got lost in our own lives, but maybe this is our chance to find our way back to being friends, to start again."

Friends. There was that word. Not that she wanted to date anyone right now. She had just gotten over a major breakup and had a huge upheaval going on in her career. Certainly she was not relationship material. But there was a part of her that always hated him only referring to them as friends. Still, there was a sense of relief washing over her. The words that had been unspoken between them had been given voice. The pain of her recent losses still lingered, but she felt a flicker of hope that maybe Noah was right. Maybe things would work out in the end.

They continued their search in a comfortable silence, occasionally showing each other one of their finds. A piece of blue glass here, a piece of frosted white glass there. As the morning wore on, Tara realized that maybe this was what she needed. A simple moment that provided a glimpse of her past that could perhaps guide her to her future. She hadn't known that she needed that. Having Noah's presence beside her was a quiet reassurance, a reminder that no matter the years or the distance, sometimes bonds remained unbroken.

CHAPTER 6

*J*ulie woke up that morning to Dawson laying in the bed beside her, staring at her. She didn't know how long he had been watching her sleep, but it was something that he did occasionally.

"What are you doing?" she asked, laughing.

"Waiting for you to wake up."

"Is there a particular reason why?"

He smiled impishly. "Well, I have a little surprise for you today. I need you to get up and get dressed. And we're running late, so hurry it up, lady." He got up quickly and disappeared into the bathroom.

Julie was completely confused. She didn't know what was going on. Thankfully, Dylan was gone to a week-long summer camp before the heat of summer set in, so it was just her and Dawson. She had no idea what he was planning.

She got up and got ready, and within thirty minutes she was standing down by the front door. He walked down the stairs, a big grin on his face, and a piece of black fabric in his hand.

"I'm going to need you to wear this."

"Is that a blindfold?" Julie asked, her mouth dropping open.

"It definitely is."

"I don't like the looks of this, Dawson," she said, putting her hands on her hips.

"You have to trust me." She sighed, and he put the soft fabric around her head and gently over her eyes, plunging her into a world of darkness. "Just trust me, Julie. I've got a surprise for you."

If this was anyone else, she would think it was the beginning of a horror movie, but she trusted her husband one-hundred percent.

The ride in his truck was a blur of muffled sounds and the occasional gentle turn. Once or twice, they hit a divot in the dirt road or a pothole, and it was jarring because she couldn't see where they were going. Her heart raced with anticipation and a bit of nervousness. She had no idea where he was taking her. He had convinced her to take a couple of days off of work and get some rest because she seemed so tired and stressed out. Of course, he had no idea that it had nothing to do with work.

She felt his steady hand guiding her as they got out of the truck. After a few cautious steps, they stopped, and he carefully removed the blindfold. She blinked her eyes a few times trying to adjust to the light. That's when the surroundings came into focus. She was standing in the middle of the most beautiful spa. Everything looked so luxurious, from the waterfall coming down one of the walls to the greenery surrounding her. And then, of course, there was the beautiful spa music, which was a mixture of water sounds and birds.

She turned to see Dixie, Colleen, Meg, and Janine standing there, each of them wearing a fluffy white robe and smiling. She realized Dawson was really worried about her if he was willing to create a spa day with her favorite people.

"Oh, my goodness. I had no idea where he was taking me. I was getting a little worried."

Janine laughed. "Did you really think he was going to hurt you?"

She looked at Dawson and hugged him, pressing her cheek into his chest. "Never."

"You ladies have fun," Dawson said, waving as he made a quick exit.

"I guess he's really worried about me."

"We're all worried about you, Mom. We were going to host a family dinner, but Dawson thought this would be better," Colleen said. She herself had looked exhausted lately. Being a new mother was hard. Julie knew that better than anybody.

The fact that her husband loved her so much that he had coordinated this day filled her heart with love. She felt terrible that she had been keeping such a secret from him. She knew she could trust him with anything that was going on in her life, and she was so grateful to have him as her husband. After her first marriage had imploded from infidelity, Dawson was like a breath of fresh air.

"Where's Mom?" Julie asked.

"Grandma offered to be the babysitter today," Meg said.

"That was nice of her," Julie said smiling. Her mother loved keeping the babies.

They took her to the dressing room and got her changed into her own white fluffy robe and some cushy little flip-flop slippers. Then they started all of their treatments - facials, pedicures, manicures. Everything culminated in the most luxurious massage. When they were finished, they were taken to a relaxation room where each of them chose a chair and just laid back drinking hot tea and relaxing. The massage chairs they were given were unbelievable, and Julie vowed to buy one for her home one day.

As they chatted, the topic turned to motherhood. Julie couldn't remember who started talking about it first.

"I found it is a constant dance trying to be present in both roles, working and motherhood. Some days, maybe most days, I feel like I'm failing at both of them," Janine said.

"I'm starting to understand that feeling all too well," Colleen interjected. "It's hard not to compare myself to other moms and feel like I should have it all together. It seems like the other moms I see on the street have everything together. They've showered. They have nice clothing. Their child looks well-fed and cared for. I feel like I look like a bridge troll most of the time."

"Darlin', we all look like trolls from time to time," Dixie said, winking.

All the women laughed.

"That's just the way it is," Meg said. "I've learned that there is no perfect way to be a mother, and I struggled after I had Vivi. But each of us brings a unique love to our children that nobody else can give them. It's just hard at the beginning."

Julie chuckled. "I can tell you it's hard all the way through. I hate to break that to you. Every single level of motherhood has its own challenges. The challenges of a brand new baby," she said leaning over and squeezing Colleen's arm. "Then there are the challenges of toddlers. Then elementary age and on and on it goes. Oh, and high school," Julie said, rolling her eyes. "And even when you're grown, your mother never stops worrying about you. There's not a day that goes by that I don't wonder how you girls are doing or what I can do to help. I thought when you turned eighteen that it would get easier, but I think it gets harder."

"Oh, don't tell us that," Janine said, putting her hands over her eyes.

"Yeah. Unfortunately, it's true. Once you're a mother, you're always a mother. And your heart is worn outside of your chest for the rest of your life."

"Julie's right. I worry over my William every single day," Dixie said.

"I promise I take good care of him," Janine said, laughing.

Dixie reached over and patted her knee. "I know you do, darlin'. I surely know you do."

Motherhood wasn't the problem for Julie these days. It was her own sense of inadequacy and failure. She had felt more vulnerable in the last few months than she had probably ever felt in her life, including when her marriage fell apart. For some reason, she felt like it was time to start opening up about it.

"I've been feeling a little lost lately myself, like I'm at a crossroads."

"It's okay to feel uncertain about things. We all go through times like that," Janine said, leaning over and touching her hand. "Just remember that we're all here for you, always. We hate to see you struggle."

She smiled slightly. "I know, and I'm going to be able to share something with everyone soon, I think. It's just taking me a little time. I'm a little embarrassed about it."

"Why don't you tell us right now?" Meg asked.

"Because I think I need to share it with my husband first."

The fact that he had done all of this for her out of the worry he was experiencing made her sad. She didn't want to worry him. She didn't want to put something on his shoulders that belonged to her, so she would tell him. She would tell him as soon as possible and admit to the embarrassment that she had been a big fat failure as an author. The dream she'd had her whole life was going up in flames.

Tara's stomach was filled with a sense of anticipation, but also anxiety, as she walked into the bank. Seagrove only had one bank, so everybody banked there including her grandmother. It was nice to be in such a small town that there was only a need for one bank. No big chains, just this little community bank that had been there for decades.

The lobby was cool and air-conditioned, a prerequisite for the South Carolina Lowcountry going into the summer. It provided a brief respite from the Seagrove sun that was hanging overhead in the sky already in the early morning hours.

She walked up to one of the tellers, an older woman she slightly recognized who had been working there for as long as Tara could remember.

"Hi. I'm here to get access to my grandmother's safe deposit box. She passed away recently."

The woman's face softened. "Oh, yes, we're all

going to miss Myra. She was a wonderful woman. Baked the best chocolate cake in town, but don't tell SuAnn at Hotcakes that I said that," the woman whispered, smiling.

"Yes, she was a wonderful woman."

Tara really didn't want to do a lot of small talk right now. She just wanted to get into the safe deposit box, now that she had worked up her courage to go to the bank. She wasn't even sure why she was so nervous. It wasn't like her grandmother was going to be keeping drugs or firearms in there, but she still didn't know exactly what she could have left her.

The attorney had already told her that there was no money to be had, not that Tara cared. She had never relied on her grandmother for finances. She had always wanted to work hard and make her own way in the world. Unfortunately, that had taken her away from Seagrove for such a long time that now she felt guilty that she didn't spend enough of that time with her grandmother.

After verifying her identification and completing a couple of pieces of paperwork, the bank attendant, whose name tag said Susan, led her to the vault. There was a click sound of the security mechanism that echoed in the quiet bank, and then they were inside the vault. Susan handed her a small key and nodded and then left her in privacy. Tara sucked in a deep breath before turning the key in the lock, her heart pounding. The box slid out with a gentle scraping sound, and then she walked over and sat it on a table nearby, sitting down in front of it and staring at it.

She opened the top, and it revealed just a few personal items. Her grandmother's gold wedding band, her grandmother's bible and then a journal. It had a dark, rich leather cover on it, and it didn't look very old. She opened it up, noticing that the pages were pretty crisp and white. This wasn't something that her grandmother had kept for a long time. Tara closed the journal before she could even read a word and traced her finger over the cover knowing that this was probably one of the last things that her grandmother had touched in this life. She felt emotions welling up within her, but she certainly didn't want to dissolve into a puddle of tears right here in the middle of the bank. No, it was definitely better for her to read this at home where she could have some privacy.

Maybe it was just full of recipes. There were questions and possibilities about what it might reveal. Was this going to help her understand her grandmother better? Uncover parts of her past she had never known about? Or was it going to be instructions on how to make the county's best chocolate cake?

Tara took the items out of the box and put them into the envelope that the woman had provided earlier. She closed the box and stood up, walking out of the vault. As Susan waved from behind the counter, Tara said a quick thank you and then stepped back outside into the bright light of day. She wondered if Susan wondered what was in that box. Did the people that worked at the bank ever get to find out? That would drive her crazy. Curiosity would get her. Maybe that was why she was a journalist. She wanted to ask questions. She liked to know the details, and maybe that was why she was missing it so much right now.

Colleen decided that she and Deacon needed to get out of the house for a while. She had spent all morning doing some cleaning and trying to keep awake. She was exhausted because Deacon had kept her up all night again, seemingly unable to be soothed. She took him to the doctor this morning and asked if there was anything wrong. There wasn't. He was just being ornery, she supposed. Maybe babies had bad days too. Since it was such a beautiful day in Seagrove, she took a detour through the park, which sat in the middle of the square. There were other people there, but thankfully she could find a bench where she could just sit down and let Deacon lay in his stroller and enjoy the beautiful blue sky above. The gentle rustling of the leaves and the distant laughter of children provided a soothing backdrop as Colleen sat on the park bench.

For a while, she watched her baby son in his stroller looking at all the things around him, taking many of them in for the first time in his young life. The sun was warming her face, as she leaned back and tilted her head to one side feeling her eyelids growing heavy. The sleepless nights of a new mother and the endless days were catching up with her. As much as she tried, she couldn't keep her eyes open. She decided that maybe it was better if she just closed her eyes for a moment. Slowly, she could feel the sounds of the park fading into the background. As everything turned black, the world around her disappeared. And as much as she knew that she shouldn't fall asleep while she was sitting there with her son, she couldn't control it anymore.

She wasn't sure how long it was before a gentle hand touched her shoulder and stirred her out of her slumber. It might've been one minute or thirty minutes. She didn't know. She blinked open her eyes and allowed them to adjust for a moment before realizing it was Tucker standing over her with a look of concern on his face.

"Honey, you were out cold," he said softly, sitting down beside her. "I came to surprise you and Deacon with a little picnic for lunch when I saw you out here, but it looked like you were pretty zonked out."

Colleen quickly looked down at her phone. She had probably been asleep for no more than five minutes, but that was enough. Not that Seagrove was a place where a lot of crime happened, but anybody could have come along and snatched her son. Yet another thing to make her feel bad about herself as a new mother. She looked at her husband, rubbing her eyes, embarrassment and relief washing over her.

"I guess I was just a little more tired than I thought," she said, forcing a smile as tears suddenly filled her eyes. He put his hand on her knee.

"I've been meaning to talk to you about all of this," he said. "I know that you have been working hard as a new mom, but also at our business. I don't know how you've been juggling everything, and I realize I probably haven't been nearly as helpful as I could be."

"You're busy at work. You have to keep the company running," she said, feeling terrible that he felt guilty.

"I'm the dad. I'm supposed to be able to do that too. Your sister actually talked to me the other day about this. She was worried about you. Apparently a lot of people are."

Colleen waved her hand. "I wish everybody would stop worrying. I'm sure this is normal for a new mom. It's a tiring job."

"Well, that might be the case, but I want you to know I'm going to put a lot more effort in. I'll get up at least half of the nights. I want you to take some days off. I'll take Deacon to the office with me on days where I'm not too busy so that you can get a break, and I think we should get some extra help."

"Extra help?"

"Maybe we can get a part-time nanny who can watch him at the office when we're both busy or give us a much needed break to go somewhere on the weekend."

"I don't know about that, Tucker. That seems like overkill."

"Well, maybe just a part-time babysitter when we need it. You've got to refill your well, or you're going to be empty."

"Yeah, I was thinking about that the other day. You know that saying that says that when the airplane is going down, you have to put on your oxygen mask first or you can't help anybody?"

He nodded his head. "That's exactly right. I've been working extra hours because I wanted to make sure that we could give our son everything that he needs. But I see now that what he needs most is both of us there and present. So, I promise to be more help, Colleen. To help you more with Deacon and with the business. We're a team, and I need you to know that I plan to do my part."

She could feel her eyes welling with tears of relief and love. This man she had married was the absolute best. She didn't care what anybody said. She had found the best man available on Earth. For so many weeks, she had been too proud and possibly too afraid to ask for help, feeling like she was admitting defeat, like she was saying that she couldn't do it all on her own. But the truth was she couldn't do it all on her own. It really did take a community.

"Thank you," she said. "I guess I've been feeling so overwhelmed and I was too scared to admit it to you. I didn't want you to think less of me." He squeezed her hand and then pulled her into a tight hug.

"You're not alone, Colleen. I'm here, and you should never be scared to tell me anything. I will always think that you hung the moon."

CHAPTER 7

*T*ara sat at the kitchen table looking out over the marsh beyond her grandmother's home. She loved the views from here. They were a soothing balm for her soul. Ever since she had come back to Seagrove, she felt herself filled with questions. Should she go fight hard to get her job back or find another one? Should she stay in Seagrove and figure out a different career path? Should she sell her grandmother's house and lose the place that she called home for her entire life? There were so many questions swirling around in her head that sometimes it felt like it was all too much.

She enjoyed spending time with Noah and craved that more and more each day. Long gone were the feelings that she had as a young child of just friendship. To her dismay, she felt an even bigger attraction to him as an adult. She knew it wasn't a good thing. She didn't want to lead him on just in case she was going to leave town and go back to the city or find a job somewhere across the country. She didn't want to hurt Noah all over again, and she wasn't even sure that he was interested in her that way. He never had been in the past that she knew of. She'd always had a crush on him, but she had managed to tame it so many times just to preserve their friendship. But now, as she sat here with her grandmother's journal sitting in front of her, hesitant to open it, she knew that when she started to read, she was going to have more questions. No matter what the contents of the journal were, she would have questions about it.

She took in a deep breath and blew it out before opening to the first page.

My dearest, Tara, if you're reading this journal, then it means I have left the world behind and gone on to a better place. I started this journal when I found out that I had cancer. I know that you're probably very upset that I didn't tell you about it, but I didn't want to burden you.

I have always thought of you as a light in this world. You were the biggest piece of my heart since the day you were born, and I did not want you to carry this weight with you. This was something neither of us could have done anything about, and I preferred for you to keep thinking of me as your healthy, happy-go-lucky grandma.

Maybe that was selfish of me. Maybe you're angry about it, but I hope not. I want you to know that you've grown into such a remarkable woman. I always knew that would happen. The pages of this journal will hold some stories for you. I'm an old woman, so I like to reminisce, as you know. I'll talk about my youth, about love and loss and the dreams that shaped my own life, and I hope by sharing these things with you that maybe I'll inspire you. Maybe it'll give you hope as you forge ahead.

I'm not a self-centered woman, but I know that me leaving you behind is going to be hard. You don't have any other family, and that has always bothered me. I always worried about the day that I was going to leave, but I know that you'll do fine. You always do.

I want to tell you a story. When I was about your age, I met a man named James. He was my first love. He wasn't your grandfather, of course, but we all have a first love and sometimes we don't end up being with them. He was a sailor and had eyes the same color as the stormy sea. His laugh could light up the darkest night. We met on the pier in Seagrove one summer evening. James showed me just what it meant to love with abandon and to dream beyond the horizon. He became my best friend, and I thought we would spend our lives together, but life has its own plans sometimes. Fate can be a cruel and fickle thing.

When he was called away to sea, he never came back. I don't really understand what happened. There was an accident, something that happens when you're out at sea defending your country, I suppose. But I was left with only memories and a heart full of what ifs. I eventually found my way to your grandfather, and I loved him dearly. I wouldn't change a thing.

As I got older, I found new dreams, new joys, but I learned lessons in that young love that held me in good stead for a lifetime. One thing it taught me was to embrace life and to cherish every moment. It taught me to not waste any time with the people that we love.

I'm saying all of this because as I write this, I know you are engaged to someone. I haven't met him officially, but I'm sure he's delightful. And you're working your dream job in Atlanta, but I can't help but feel that there is something missing for you, something that I always assumed would happen naturally. But maybe I have to hurry it along. Maybe I have to help you connect the dots. It's about you and Noah.

I watched you two grow up together. Your friendship was as strong and natural as the tide coming in and out. I had always seen something special between you, some-

thing that went way deeper than friendship. It reminded me of James and me when we first met. I always had hoped that you would find your way to each other. That you would get to experience a love like I did.

Perhaps it's not my place to say, but I hope that if you ever cross paths with Noah again, you will think about these words. That before you make a lifetime commitment to someone else, you will remember what true love is and what it feels like. I was privileged to have it twice in my life. I hope for you a life filled with adventures and a love so big that your heart can barely contain it.

Also at the back of this journal, you'll find a folded piece of paper. It is a survey to a piece of land near the ocean that I purchased many years ago. I always dreamed of building something there, my little haven by the sea, but I couldn't bear to leave this home behind. So I just held onto it in case I ever wanted to use it for something in the future. I want you to think of this land as your safety net, my dear. Should life ever lead you back to Seagrove, I want you to have this piece of land to start anew, whether it is to build your own dream house or to sell it and have the money to support yourself while you figure out your next path. Do with it as you wish. I don't have any attachments to what you do with it as long as it serves you for the *future. I want it to bring you closer to joy and happiness.*

Remember that life is full of choices and chances. Don't be afraid to take either one of them. Don't be afraid to make the hard choices and take the big chances as you weave your own story. It is in those valleys that you'll find out who you really are and what you really want. The tough times sharpen us in ways that the good times cannot.

You have always been my greatest joy. In you, I have always seen strength, resilience, and a light that will carry you through your own journey. Always follow your heart. It knows the way.

Love, Grandma

T ara closed the journal. She couldn't bear to read more of it right now, choosing to let her grandmother's words absorb into her soul like a sponge. She missed her more than words could express, but she was so grateful for her written words right now. They were like a life preserver to her.

Yet again, Julie sat at her computer, staring at the blinking cursor. She knew that she needed to get back to writing. A part of her still held out a sliver of hope that one of the many agents and publishers who'd declined her would suddenly email an apology, telling her it was a mistake and they loved her book.

This was something she had always wanted to do, and she would not give up on her dream, no matter how long it took. Going to the spa had helped her in so many ways. It had given her hope that she could do this, even though she hadn't told anyone exactly what was going on. With her fingers shaking a little, she finally decided to search on how to publish a novel.

The screen was filled with articles and guides, success stories and failures. Each click opened a brand new world of possibilities and fears. She found herself knee-deep in research. After the initial intimidation she felt about self-publishing started to finally dissipate, she felt empowered, encouraged, excited. By publishing her own book, she didn't have to wait around for an agent or a publishing company to accept her. She could take the reins and publish her own book, do her own marketing, and make more money in the process. The path would definitely not be easy, and she had a ton to learn, but she realized that she could do it. She had done a lot of hard things in her life.

Lost in her exploration, she didn't hear Dawson enter the room. He was standing in the doorway when she turned to look, leaning against it with his shoulder, a soft smile on his face. She loved when she saw him doing that. One of the first times she'd met him was when he was leaning against a doorframe with that lazy smile and his cute little dimple.

"What are you working on?" he asked, stepping into the room. She was excited but anxious to finally tell him what was going on.

"Sit down," she said, pointing at an armchair across the room. He sat down and she turned her rolling desk chair toward him.

"Is everything okay?"

"Yes, everything's fine. I just think it's time I finally tell you what's been going on." A look of relief washed over his face.

"Thank goodness. I've been so worried. I can't help you deal with something if I don't know what it is."

"So, you know I've always wanted to write a novel."

"Of course. You've talked about it a lot, almost ever since the day I met you."

"Well, I've been working on it now for a couple of years."

"What?" he said, his mouth dropping open. "When did you have the time? I mean, between running the bookstore, being a grandma, being a new mother to Dylan, being my wife, helping with the inn... When were you writing?"

"Sometimes I would get up in the early morning before you woke up, or I would do it on breaks when I was at the bookstore. A couple of times, I even got up to write while you were asleep at night. I write on my phone when I'm waiting for appointments or at Dylan's games..."

"Wow. I must not be very observant," Dawson said, laughing. "So, why didn't you want to tell me that?"

"That's not all of it. Not only did I write it, but I submitted it to several publishers. I tried to get an agent. For the last several weeks, I've been checking the mail every day, getting rejections. Some of them have been email rejections. I've just been getting rejected all over the place," she said, laughing. It wasn't funny, but she didn't want him to see her upset.

"Honey, you know that some of the biggest authors in the world got tons of rejections. So many of them didn't see success at first."

"I know, but I've also now realized that I'm just not built for that."

"You can't give up," he said, walking toward her and kneeling down in front of her, taking her hands.

"I'm not going to give up," she said, so thankful that she had a husband who cared like that. "I've decided that I'm going to self-publish it."

His eyes widened. "Oh, that's a great idea. I didn't even think of that."

"I didn't at first either. I guess I just wanted to go the more traditional route and have it published by some big publisher, but I'm realizing that I really don't need somebody else to tell me that my novel is good. I only care if readers think it's good. And by self-publishing it, I can get it right into their hands."

"You're definitely right. You don't need anybody else to validate you, Julie. You're one of the strongest women I know. You can do this, and I'll be there to help you. I'm so glad that you finally told me."

"I'm sorry that it took me so long. I was just embarrassed."

He looked shocked. "Embarrassed? Why would you be embarrassed to tell me? I'm your husband."

"I didn't want to tell anybody. Dixie was the only one who got it out of me. I'm sorry I didn't tell you first. I just didn't want you to see me as a failure."

He stood up and pulled her out of the chair and closer to him, resting her cheek against his chest. "I could never think that you were a failure, because you're not a failure. I know you're going to get this novel out there and readers are going to love it. And I'm going to celebrate you and cheer you on the whole time."

Tara sat in her grandmother's favorite chair, the evening sun going down quickly in the sky. She had been reading the journal for several hours now, learning all kinds of things that she had never known about her grandmother.

One example was her grandmother's description of working as a typist when she was fifteen years old. She'd left school at that age, never graduating, because she felt she needed to help her parents financially. The male-dominated office was a hard place for a young girl to work, especially in the 1960s. Her days were filled with tapping away on the keys, transcribing letters and documents and trying to keep the men from touching her. Once, when her boss tried to do just that, she'd smashed his hand with a stapler and gotten fired.

Tara was so impressed by the toughness of her grandmother. Women were built differently back in those days. They had to be tough. The world wasn't doing them any favors.

The house was quiet except for the occasional creak of the wooden floors, as if the walls were leaning in to listen to all the tales her grandmother wrote in the pages of the journal. As she turned each page, they crackled softly under her fingers. She loved to look at her grandmother's handwriting as it flowed across the paper. She had that old kind of cursive writing that people couldn't do anymore. It gave her a tangible connection to the past that felt both intimately close and so very distant. Tara started to read and could hear her grandmother's voice audibly in her mind. The entries were very different from page to page as if her grandmother was trying to lay out her entire history so that she didn't get forgotten when she passed away from this earth.

Little did she know that Tara could never forget her. She thought about her almost every moment of the day. Maybe that would lessen as the years went on, but she knew there would never be a day that would go by where she wouldn't draw on the strength of the woman who had raised her.

The entries in the journal painted all sorts of vivid pictures of her grandmother as a young woman who was full of dreams and had a zest for life. She wrote about meeting James at the pier in more depth, talked about their conversations, their hopes, and their dreams. Tara could almost see them like they were two characters from some romance novel, but they were really just silhouettes against a setting sun in the Lowcountry.

As she turned more pages, the tone would shift with longing and sadness, talking about how he had left for sea, how she had loved him so much and waited for a return that never happened. She also talked about her love for Tara's grandfather, Bob, and how they met. The love seemed to be equal for him as well, and she was so thankful that her grandmother got to experience it twice in her life. She wondered if she would experience it at all.

She felt a pang of sadness for herself, not for her grandmother's lost love as much as for her own. She had never had a love that was so important that losing it would tear her up like it did her grandmother. In fact, she hardly thought at all about her breakup with her fiancé. It felt more like a failure than it did heartbreak, and that alone was heartbreaking enough.

Her grandmother also wrote more about how she found the plot of land and what she had planned to do with it at several points during her lifetime. She said the place instantly felt like a part of her soul, and she had hoped that one day she would have a home sitting on that very spot. It wasn't just a piece of property to her grandmother. It was a legacy, something that she could pass down to Tara to do with what she wanted. She hoped that Tara would use that piece of land to help herself get a leg up in life and build the life of her dreams, that it might serve as a foundation. It was so strange how her grandmother seemed to know exactly what she needed, even though she was suffering through her own last days on earth. She had not told her about the breakup or the job loss, yet her grandmother seemed to intuitively know she was going to need this.

Tara closed the journal when her eyes started to get too tired to stay open. She felt like she needed a little nap before dinner, and she was going to allow that for herself. She wasn't an old person, not just yet, but she felt like if you needed a nap, you should take one. So she put the journal on the table, leaned her head back in the chair and closed her eyes. She was going to need to go visit the land and see where it was, but for now, she wasn't going to think about anything else except getting some rest and then cooking herself some dinner.

CHAPTER 8

Tara felt a bit nervous, and she didn't know why. It wasn't like she hadn't known Noah her entire life, but when he had invited her to come to a showing of his art at a local gallery, she was surprised.

The evening was balmy in Seagrove as most were in summer. There was a gentle breeze whispering through the streets, flowing through the Spanish moss hanging in the trees overhead. She met Noah outside the gallery. The building was lit up with a soft, welcoming glow, and she could hear the muted conversations and music as it spilled out onto the sidewalk. Noah was in a casual shirt and jeans and greeted her with an excited smile. He always had a good smile, even as a kid. It lit up the room.

"Thanks for coming. It means so much that you agreed to be here," he said.

"Why wouldn't I? Of course I would never miss it. I can't wait to see your work on display."

They went into the gallery, and the walls were adorned with all kinds of artwork from other local artisans. Vibrant colors and striking forms drew the eye. Noah's pieces were displayed prominently. His sea glass artistic creations transforming the ocean's discarded treasures into beautiful, intricate things. They moved through the crowd with Noah explaining the inspiration behind each of his pieces anytime someone came to look. Tara listened intently, admiring his talent. She was not an artistic person in the least. She was great with words, but she couldn't possibly paint something and certainly couldn't make anything out of sea glass. She had seen it as a beautiful part of the ocean, but obviously Noah had seen it for so much more.

When they came up to a particularly stunning piece, which was a large mosaic depicting the Seagrove shoreline, Noah looked at Tara. "This one is special to me," he said. "It's inspired by a memory. One of the many days that we spent on the beach as kids."

"Really? How do you remember something like that?"

He smiled slightly. "It was actually when we were in high school. We had gone out there early one morning, and I remember you talking about how beautiful the sky was that day. We only had a few weeks left of high school, and I knew you were going to be leaving soon for college. It was breaking my heart, so I remember that day particularly well."

Breaking his heart? She was shocked to hear him say such a thing. Why would it break his heart that she left for college? At that time, they had planned on remaining friends and staying in touch. Even though that didn't happen, a broken heart seemed to be a big phrase for a friend going off to college. She decided not to press further. This was his night. It was important for him to stay focused.

"It's so beautiful Noah. You really captured the essence of the Seagrove shoreline so perfectly," she said, looking at the shades of blue, green and sandy beige sea glass. She also felt a wave of nostalgia as she thought about those moments, although she didn't remember this particular one. They stood there in silence for a moment staring at it, words not passing between them, hanging in the air like a thick fog.

"I need to confess something," he said, looking nervous. Tara's heart skipped a beat. Was he going to profess his love for her?

"What?"

"You asked me before if I had saved any sea glass from when we were kids, and I said no. I didn't want you to think that I was some kind of weirdo who saved pieces of sea glass just because you had found them."

Her eyes widened. "You saved my sea glass?"

He smiled slightly. "This piece is yours, Tara. All of these are pieces you found and gave to me. It's not for sale, actually. I just brought it to show you."

Her eyes welled with tears. "Really? Why would you do that, Noah? Save those pieces?"

He cleared his throat and lowered his voice since people were walking around the gallery. "Because I missed you so much. Having this piece in my house all these years reminded me of better times. It has moved with me everywhere. Trust me, my ex-wife had questions about why I wouldn't get rid of it."

"Wow. I don't know what to say."

"I want you to have it."

"No. I can't possibly take this. It means so much to you."

"It's time for you to have it. To give you a connection to Seagrove."

"And to you," she said, softly.

"Maybe that's my ulterior motive," he said, smiling slightly. What did all of this mean?

"Thank you. I will treasure it always. It's the most beautiful piece of artwork I've ever seen."

"Tara, having you here and seeing my work through your eyes, well, it's made this evening so much more special."

She looked at him and felt a connection that went beyond friendship. She didn't know if he felt it, too, but she suspected something was going on. "I'm so glad to be here, Noah. Your art, it's just beautiful, and it tells a story that no one else can tell."

He looked at her and quietly said, "Our story."

Julie sat at the table outside the cafe waiting for Colleen and Meg to meet her for lunch. She had sworn Dawson to secrecy because she wanted to share with her daughters exactly what had been going on. She knew they had been worried about her, and she felt terribly guilty about that. As a mother, it was her job to make sure that her kids weren't worried about her. She was supposed to be the adult, even though they were both adults and mothers themselves. She saw them walking closer, waving. Vivi was not with Meg today as she was at a play date with one of Christian's co-workers at the college.

Colleen also didn't have Deacon with her. She had told Julie that Tucker was going to be taking care of Deacon a little more regularly and taking him to work on days he wasn't very busy, so she assumed that's where he was. In fact, Colleen looked so much better rested than she had recently.

"Hey Mom," Meg said, leaning over and hugging her mom really quickly before sitting down. Colleen hugged her and sat down in the other chair.

"You look so rested," Julie said to Colleen, reaching over and touching her cheek.

"Thank you. I'm finally getting some sleep. When Tucker found me dozing off in the park, I was embarrassed, but it was a good wake-up call. No pun intended."

"Yeah, we really don't need you sleeping in the park," Meg said. "People might get the wrong idea."

Julie laughed. "Well, I'm glad that he's helping out. I know he would've helped out if he had just known what was going on."

Meg looked at her mother, "So, we want to know what's been going on with you."

Before Julie could say anything, the waitress came over to the table and took their order. When she finally walked away, Julie took in a deep breath and blew it out.

"Okay, I'm about to tell you what's been going on."

"Spill the tea," Meg said. Julie just stared at her.

"I don't know what that means."

"Oh, Mom, it's lingo that the younger kids use these days. It just means tell us the gossip. You really have to get with the program," Colleen laughed at her sister.

"Okay, so you know, I've been wanting to write a novel."

"You wrote a novel?" Colleen said, full of energy.

"Well, yes. I've been writing it for a couple of years now."

"A couple of years?" Meg said, her eyebrows furrowing. "And you didn't tell us?"

"No, because I didn't know if I would ever even finish it. But I did, and I think it's pretty good."

"So, why would you keep that a secret?" Colleen asked.

"Well, because I submitted it to some agents and

publishers, and I got rejections every time. Like lots of them. It was embarrassing."

"You know that happens," Meg said. "We have lots of books in our store that probably went through tons of rejections before they got published."

"Well, what I've learned is that I can't take it. That's too much stress."

"You're giving up? You're not going to publish your novel?" Colleen asked.

"No, I'm not giving up. Dixie gave me the idea of self-publishing it, so that's what I'm researching right now."

"Oh, that's fantastic, Mom," Meg said, clapping her hands. "We have lots of self-published novels in the bookstore, and some of them sell really well."

"It's a lot more work from what I understand. I'll have to do my own marketing. I'll have to hire people to do covers and formatting and editing, but I think I can do it."

"I *know* you can do it," Colleen said reaching over and squeezing her hand. "And we'll help you. We're good at organizing events. You can have book sign-ings at the bookstore, and I know Tucker would be glad to help you with some of the ads that you can do on social media. He does them all the time for the toy company."

"I'm so thankful that I have such a strong community and family around me," Julie said, reaching out and taking both of their hands. "I knew I should have told you earlier. I was just having such a hard time dealing with feeling like a failure."

"You're never going to be a failure in our eyes, Mom," Meg said. "You're the strongest woman we know. You've rebuilt your life from a really bad time, and look what you've got. This is like a dream life for most people."

Julie smiled, "It's a dream life for me."

Tara stood at the edge of the plot of land right near the beach. She had brought Noah with her because it just seemed right that she had someone there who cared about her and her grandmother to help make a decision on what to do with the land. It wasn't a huge piece of land as most lots near the beach weren't, but it was big enough for a house or maybe even a couple of houses. The untamed beauty took her breath away. The ocean breeze was constant while the wild grasses swayed gently, and in the distance she could hear the waves providing a natural soundtrack for their visit.

"Well, this is it," Tara said, her voice full of awe. "This is the land that my grandmother bought. I can't believe she owned this, and I didn't know it."

Noah looked around, taking in the unspoiled view. "It's really incredible, Tara. There's so much potential here. You could build a house, build a family here."

"Or I could sell it," Tara said. "Take the money and start a new life."

Noah chuckled. "You act like you're going into the witness protection program."

She smiled. "No, but it is worth a lot of money as you well know, being right here on the ocean. It's pretty rare in this area."

"That's true, but you wouldn't want to build a house here?"

"I don't know. That would cost a lot of money to build, and I don't have access to that kind of money right now. On top of that, I'm not sure I want to move out of my grandmother's house. I grew up there. I love it."

"I know you do."

They began to walk around the perimeter of the lot, mostly taking in the ocean breeze and the waves.

Every time Tara was at the beach, she felt more serene. She didn't feel that way back in the city, although she had loved where she lived. She had loved her job. She tried not to think about it.

This lot was a blank canvas. Maybe she could hold onto it for a few years and then finally afford to build her own dream home, but would it be a dream home? Every time she thought of home, she thought of her grandma's house.

"Remember how we used to explore that area over there when we were kids?" Noah asked, pointing off into the distance. "We were adventurers, weren't we?"

"Yes, we were."

"We always found an adventure no matter where we were. Remember all the forts we built and the secret clubhouses?" He laughed. A long moment passed between them as they just stared out into the ocean.

Finally, Tara spoke up. "Do you have any regrets?"

"What do you mean?"

"I mean, do you ever think back on that time of our lives and regret anything?"

"Do you?"

"I regret that I didn't stay in touch with you like I promised. I got so wrapped up in school and then my climb up the career ladder that I let one of the most special people in my life go. What about you?"

He stood there awkwardly for a moment before slightly turning toward her. "Yes, there is something I regret in a big way."

She turned to face him. "Really? What is it?"

"I regret that I never did this."

Before she could say another word, he moved closer, putting his hands on her cheeks and pressing his lips to hers. Tara felt like she was in a tornado. Everything whirling around her. She couldn't hear the waves. She couldn't feel the breeze. All she could feel was his lips on hers. When he finally pulled back, he stared at her searching her eyes, looking both worried and happy at the same time. Tara didn't know what to say. She just stood there with her mouth hanging open.

"Noah, I don't understand."

"I'm sorry. I shouldn't have done that," he said and stepped back, holding up his hands as if he was putting up some kind of force field between them.

"No, don't be sorry. I just don't understand."

"What don't you understand, Tara?"

"You've never had any interest in me like that."

"Who says?"

She put her hands on her hips. "Wait, a minute.

You mean this entire time you liked me like *that*?"

"Of course I did. I thought I was giving off all the signals and then you went off to college, and I never heard from you again."

"I know. I told you I'm sorry. Life just got really busy and…"

"No, I'm not blaming you. I'm just telling you that I never thought you were interested."

Her mouth dropped open again. "I flirted with you from the day I met you. I swear men can be so dense sometimes."

He laughed and walked toward her again, dropping the imaginary force field. He put his hands on her upper arms and looked her in the eye. "I have been in love with you since we were kids." Another long silence. She didn't know what to say. Somebody could have knocked her over with a feather.

"Why didn't you tell me?"

"Why didn't *you* tell *me*?" he asked.

"I was afraid. I didn't think you liked me that way, and I didn't want to ruin our friendship."

"Same," he said.

"So, we wasted all these years?"

"It looks that way," he said, dropping his arms. "I guess I should have been brave enough to tell you before you left."

"I should have told you."

"Well, all we have is right now. You're here in Seagrove. Maybe we still have a chance."

She smiled sadly. "I don't know, Noah. I never want to lose touch again. I always want to be friends, but I can't promise that I'm staying in Seagrove. I have a career that I love, and I would like to get back to it at some point. I can't really pursue it in Seagrove, you know?"

"I understand, but I don't want to have any more regrets, Tara. While you're here, can we just give it a try? Go out on a real date?"

She stood there for a moment, and then a smile spread across her face. "You're asking me on a date?"

"Yes, I am," he said, smiling back.

"Well, I can't say no to that."

Colleen sat at her kitchen table, nervous. There was a stack of resumes in front of her, and Meg sat in the chair next to her being supportive and ready to help interview candidates for the part-time nanny position for little Deacon. They would only be hiring a nanny for a few hours each week, just so Colleen could get out of the house, run some errands, go to the office, and help her husband with work. She felt terrible hiring somebody because she felt like she didn't really need it, but thankfully she had the resources to do it, at least for a few months. She wanted to hire somebody that was trustworthy and who would take care of Deacon just like she did, and she was beginning to worry that she wasn't going to find anybody like that.

The first candidate was a young woman named Emily. She arrived on time, was in her early twenties, and had a bright smile. She sat down in front of Colleen and Meg to begin the interview.

"So, Emily, can you tell me a little about your experience with children?" Colleen asked, trying to mask her nervousness. She needed to seem confident.

"Well, I've been babysitting since I was about fifteen, so I have experience with kids of all ages. Right now, I'm studying early childhood education in college because I am planning to become a teacher," she said enthusiastically. She had a lot of energy for this early in the morning.

Meg nodded, "That's great. Now, tell me how would you handle a situation where Deacon is being particularly fussy?" Meg was a no-nonsense kind of person. She was going to ask very pointed questions, Colleen knew that much.

"Well, I believe in gentle, patient care, and there's always a reason behind the fussiness. I would need to figure out whether Deacon needed his diaper changed, whether he's hungry or maybe tired, and then it's just about comforting and taking care of his immediate needs."

Colleen and Meg quickly exchanged a look of approval. As the interview continued, Emily's responses were always thoughtful and confident. When she left, Colleen felt more hopeful.

The next candidate was a middle-aged woman named Evelyn. She was more reserved, but she had a lot more experience.

"I've raised three of my own children, and I've worked as a part-time nanny for the past ten years." Her voice was very calm and reassuring. Meg asked about her approach to childcare and Evelyn smiled, "Well, it's always about love and patience. Every kid is different, so you have to understand their needs. That's critical, and of course, provide a safe and nurturing environment."

As the interview went on, Colleen continued to feel a calmness wash over her. Evelyn's experience and gentle nature were evident. She even attended the same church as Dixie, and her answers resonated with the way that Colleen viewed childcare.

When Evelyn left, Colleen turned to Meg, "You know, this is harder than I thought. Emily is definitely qualified and has tons of energy, but Evelyn is so experienced and calming."

Meg nodded, "Both would be great candidates, but it's about who you feel most comfortable with. You have to trust your instincts. That's the most important thing as a mother. You know what's best for Deacon."

Colleen took a deep breath and mulled over the interviews looking at everybody's resumes once again. Both candidates had their strengths, but she was definitely leaning towards one. She knew that this was the first step to balancing her new role as a mother and entrepreneur. She could do both well, but she might need help. A little while later, she picked up her phone and sent a text to the new nanny. It would be Evelyn. She just felt more comfortable with her because of her experience. After she sent the text, she set her phone on the kitchen table, took a sip of her hot cup of coffee, and smiled.

CHAPTER 9

*J*ulie and Dawson walked into the quaint little print shop in town. This was one of the most exciting days of her life. She couldn't wait to see her book in printed form. She had already done the prep work for putting her book online, but she needed to do this extra step to get some printed copies to use for local book signings.

The shop was filled with the scent of ink and paper. She clutched her manuscript tightly to her chest, even though she had already sent an electronic version to the owner of the print shop. There was a mixture of excitement and nerves flowing through her body.

The shop's owner, Mr. Henderson, greeted them with a warm smile.

"Dawson, Julie, glad you could come. I got your email with your novel, and I've already done some mock-ups, if you'd like to see them."

Julie was so excited. She had hoped that he would've printed something up, given that she had sent him the cover that she'd had designed just days ago. Choosing from all the different options from her cover designer was so much fun, yet so daunting. Books were judged by their covers, and she wanted to make sure that hers accurately reflected the story and also got readers to want to pick it up.

"Come on around the counter and let me show you some things."

Dawson and Julie walked around and stood next to Mr. Henderson, who pulled a book from under the counter. She couldn't believe that she was seeing it in real life.

"Now, I printed it in the typical mass-market, paperback size, but we can do a little larger if you'd like," he said, handing it over. As Julie clutched it in her hands, she felt her eyes start to water. She looked up at Dawson.

"Can you believe this is my book? I wrote this," she said, excitement in her voice. "I swear I never thought I would see it actually printed. Thank you so much, Mr. Henderson."

"You're very welcome."

Dawson put his arm around her and squeezed her close.

"I'm so proud of you," he said in her ear.

"This looks wonderful, but I do think I'd like it to be just a bit bigger."

"That's no problem. We just need to work out how many copies you want, and I can give you some pricing."

"That would be wonderful."

"And I'll tell you what. Why don't you keep that copy for your collection," he said winking at her. She almost wanted to give him a hug, but since she had just met him, she thought that might be inappropriate.

"Thank you so much. I will treasure this forever."

After they finished talking about some of the other details, Julie and Dawson walked outside, hand in hand.

"You're doing it. You're making your dream a reality," he said, smiling at her.

She felt a sense of fulfillment. She was always proud of the things that she had done; leaving a bad marriage, becoming an owner at the bookstore, raising two wonderful girls, adopting her son. But she was very proud of this accomplishment. She had wanted to do it her whole life, but she hadn't ever thought she was good enough to write a book. She didn't think she was smart enough, creative enough. And now as she held her very own book in her hand, she knew that she had started to fulfill one of the biggest dreams of her life.

In the past few days, Tara had found that spending time with Noah was the thing she looked forward to most each day. She still had no idea what she was doing with her career, and she hadn't decided about selling the land or keeping it. She just knew that she felt comfortable in Seagrove and especially comfortable with Noah.

They had gotten closer and closer as the days passed, seeing each other each and every day, either for lunch or breakfast. Sometimes she went over to his shop and spent some time just sitting with him, chatting while customers came in and out. She had even gotten to see him do some of his work on a few custom orders, and she was impressed as always with his creativity and talent.

When she thought back on how those years she'd had such a crush on him and had no idea he felt the same, it drove her a little nuts. All those years. All that time. All those relationships that weren't quite right because her heart belonged to someone else. A part of her felt regret, but then she knew that everything had led her here, anyway. Maybe this was the way it was supposed to be. Maybe they weren't meant to be high school sweethearts, but fate still pushed them back together, anyway.

Tonight, they were finally going on their first official date. They strolled hand in hand along the quaint streets of Seagrove, walking toward a new Cuban restaurant that had recently opened by the water. The evening air was balmy, carrying with it the gentle scent of the sea as fading sunlight was casting a warm golden hue over the whole town. Sunset was her favorite time in the Lowcountry. The restaurant, which was aptly named Havana Breeze, stood out with its vibrant colors and lively music. As they walked toward the front door, Tara could hear the rhythm of the music, which was a blend of salsa and jazz. He opened the door for her as most Southern men did, and led her inside with his hand gently resting on the small of her back.

The inside was a beautiful tapestry of rich, warm colors, and the walls were adorned with vintage

Cuban posters. The shelves were lined with colorful glass bottles and dimly lit lanterns were hanging from the ceiling. They were seated at a cozy table in the corner by the window with a beautiful view of the marsh beyond. The water reflected the colors of the setting sun, turning the scene outside into a moving painting. As they looked at the menu, Noah's hand found Tara's on the table, their fingers intertwining. She felt a surge of warmth every time he touched her that deepened with every shared memory or smile. She couldn't believe they had spent so many years apart. How much time was wasted? She tried not to think about it. Maybe if they had gotten together as teenagers or young adults, things wouldn't have worked out. Who knows? She knew that she was meant to work in the journalism field, so she was glad that she had gone to college and started her career. But a part of her felt sad that they had missed so much time together.

They decided to start with an appetizer of tostones, which were fried plantains that were served with a special homemade garlic dipping sauce. Noah ordered Ropa Vieja, which is a traditional Cuban dish of slow cooked, shredded beef in a tomato sauce. Tara chose Camarones al Ajillo, which was shrimp sauteed in a garlic and lime sauce.

They waited for their food as the conversation flowed effortlessly. Noah stared into Tara's eyes when she talked, listening to every word she said, like it was the most important thing he'd ever heard. She found herself sometimes lost in his gaze, the rest of the world around them just fading into the background.

When the food arrived, the flavors and aromas filled the air around them. Each dish was a true masterpiece. They had such rich, bold flavors with Cuba coming to life in every bite. The music around them kept their feet tapping during the entire meal. It truly was the perfect kind of date where you get to be with somebody you really like while enjoying beautiful music and food.

"Care to dance?" Noah asked, holding out his hand across the table.

"Seriously? There's no dance floor!"

"Who needs a dance floor?"

Tara smiled and took his hand, standing up. They moved to a small spot beside their table as Noah pulled her close. She slid her arms around his neck, something she'd wanted to do at every school dance they'd ever gone to together. His hands held her tightly at the waist as they moved in time with the music, looking at each other. Tara didn't care that there wasn't a dance floor, anyway. She only cared that Noah was pressed against her, holding her tightly.

After they finished dinner, Noah suggested that they take a walk down by the waterfront. The moon was now reflecting off the water, which cast a silvery light on their path. He continued holding her hand firmly as they walked, and she couldn't imagine ever holding anyone else's hand. Even when they were kids, they had never held hands, but it just felt so natural and right. They talked about all kinds of things from Tara's breakup to what happened with her job. She also talked about her college days and how she got into working in television. He talked about all the different paths his life had taken before opening his art shop. It was just an enjoyable, relaxing conversation with someone that she could spend hours talking to.

"How did you meet your ex-wife?"

"Well, we met at the grocery store, believe it or not. She needed something off a high shelf…"

"And you're pretty tall," Tara said, smiling as she looked at him.

"Yep. Anyway, we chatted for a long time in the pasta aisle, and I asked her on a date."

"How long were you married?"

"Almost six years."

"What happened?"

He shrugged his shoulders. "It was just one of those things where you fall out of love. For most people it happens after decades. For us, we knew after five years, I guess. We separated for a few months, and instead of getting back together, she got engaged to a man she met at a different grocery store."

Tara stopped in her tracks. "What?"

"I'm totally serious. He was a store manager who gave her the price on some cookies. They got married six days after our divorce was final."

"Wow. That's quite a story," she said, starting to walk again. "I'm sorry."

Noah laughed. "Don't be sorry. If that hadn't happened, I wouldn't be walking around Seagrove holding your hand." He stopped and pulled her in front of him, leaning down and kissing the top of her head. "And I wouldn't want to be anywhere else."

As they reached her door, the night had gotten darker and there were stars twinkling in the clear sky. Noah turned to Tara as they approached her front door, and she could see the reflection of moonlight in his eyes. Slowly, he leaned in, his lips meeting hers, a gentle kiss, but filled with passion at the same time. When he pulled away, they kept their foreheads resting against each other. "Goodnight Tara," he said in a soft voice.

"Goodnight, Noah," she said before she watched him walk down the sidewalk, looking back and winking at her one more time. Yes, this was going to get complicated.

J ulie had been in her home office all morning, working on learning new formatting software so she could get her book ready to become an ebook. She was going to be publishing it today. Dawson had gone to work because she had asked him to, wanting to be alone when she finally clicked that button to send her book off into cyberspace.

As her finger hovered over the mouse ready to click the publish button, she thought about what this meant. What if readers hated her book? What if they thought it was the worst thing they had ever read? She had such imposter syndrome sometimes. Still, she had put her heart and soul into this manuscript, and she was going to put it out into the world and just see what happened. Even if everything completely failed, she still had the love of her family and friends to hold her up. She would be very dejected, of course, but she would be able to move on knowing that she had finally at least accomplished her life's dream of publishing a novel.

Her heart raced with a mix of excitement and nerves. This was the moment that she'd been working toward for so long. The culmination of all the hours of writing, revising and dreaming. She sucked in a deep breath and then blew it out through pursed lips. As she clicked the button, the page refreshed with a message that confirmed that her book was now being approved for publishing. It would be just a few hours before it would probably go live on all the major online retailers. She felt such a sense of accomplishment. Her eyes welling up with tears of joy and relief. She had done it. She had published her novel.

Just as she was about to allow the tears to spill over, Dylan came walking into the room behind her. He was home for the summer and looking for something to do, so he was constantly wandering around the house.

"Hey, Mom. What are you doing?"

"Well, I just did something very important. I published my very first book."

"You did? So, it's out there for people to buy right now?"

"Well, it will be in a few hours. It takes a little bit of time for it to be approved through the system."

"Congratulations!" Dylan said, walking over and hugging her tightly around the neck. Adopting him out of the foster care system had been one of the biggest blessings of her life. Dylan was like a ball of love. She worried how he would change when he became a teenager soon. Would he act like her daughters did for a while where he was embarrassed by her very existence. Those were tough years.

"What are you up to right now?" Julie asked her son, pushing some hair back that was hanging in his eyes. She really needed to take him to get a haircut soon.

"I was wondering if I can go over to Eric's house to hang out for a while?"

"Sure, that's fine. Does Eric's mother know you're coming?"

"Yes. She's the one who told him to invite me," he said smiling. She was so happy that he had made some good friends at school, and most of them only lived right down the road. He could walk or ride his bike to all of their houses. Seagrove was a small, safe community where everybody watched out for each other. If a mother was anywhere around, she was watching everybody else's kids, too. It was kind of a throwback to the good old days.

"Okay, but be careful and watch for cars. You're riding your bike?"

"Yes, ma'am," he said, nodding his head.

"Okay, go ahead then. But be back by five to help set the table for dinner," she called out.

As she heard Dylan running down the hallway toward the stairs, she turned back to the computer and refreshed the screen again. Her book still wasn't approved yet, but she knew it would be soon, according to the people she had talked to in Facebook groups who had already self-published books.

She decided that maybe she would go do some of her housework and prepare some food for the rest of the week. When she had first met Dawson, he had a wonderful woman named Lucy working for him. Lucy had worked with the family for many years going back as far as his grandmother. She had cooked and cleaned and helped to take care of the guests when the inn was open. But a couple of years ago, Lucy had decided to retire and move closer to family. They still heard from her every now and again, usually through email.

That meant that Julie had to take on the responsibility of making sure that the inn was taken care of and that food was always made and ready. They had closed down to new guests for the last few weeks just because she was so stressed out with her book and work, but they were going to be opening again soon for the summer rush. In fact, they already had some reservations for next weekend.

As she tidied up the house and tried to get her mind off of her book, she found herself going back to the office over and over again, refreshing the screen. First, she saw that her book got approved. Then an hour or so later, she could actually see it up on one of the major book retailer websites. She kept trying to distract herself, drinking a cup of coffee, grabbing a doughnut. Before she knew it, she was stuffed full of junk food and coffee and she could feel her hands trembling slightly.

She continued refreshing the screen, hoping against hope that somebody would order her book. It didn't make any sense, really. She hadn't marketed it or advertised it yet, but she still had hope that she would see that one first sale soon. Finally, she decided to close her computer because she was driving herself crazy. She wasn't going to let a slow start dampen her spirit. Whether her book sold hundreds or thousands of copies or sold just one, she knew that she had achieved something incredible that most people never got to do, and for that she was appreciative.

Tara sat on the living room sofa with her laptop in her lap. This morning, she had just been scrolling the internet, looking at social media. Every so often, she would think about somebody she went to school with and then look them up to see if she could find them on Facebook or some other social media platform. Her mind, of course, was occasionally drifting to Noah, thinking about the wonderful weeks they'd spent together and rediscovering each other as they deepened their bond. It was almost like no time had passed since childhood. Everything felt new and exciting even though they had known each other practically their whole lives.

All of a sudden, her phone rang, which broke her out of the peaceful silence and actually startled her a bit. She didn't recognize the number, but she could see that it was coming from Atlanta. Her curiosity was piqued, so she answered.

"Hello?"

"Hi. Is this Tara?" a professional voice on the other end asked.

"Yes. This is Tara," she said. Her heart starting to speed up a bit. Was this someone calling about legal implications of what happened at her last job? Was she about to get sued? She had no idea who would be calling her or why.

"Hi. This is Jenna from The Chronicle. We understand that you are available for work, and we'd like to talk to you about possibly coming on as a staff writer."

She froze in place. How did this woman know she had lost her job? "I'm sorry. I'm confused. I didn't apply for any jobs."

Jenna chuckled under her breath. "Yes, but you know that the journalism community in Atlanta is actually quite small. We all seem to know each other. Some friends told me that you were available, and they raved about your qualifications, so I would like to talk to you about coming on board with us."

"As you can imagine, this is kind of surprising. I wasn't expecting any job offers today."

"I understand. I'd be glad to send you some additional information. I think it's a very good position, and with your background and experience, you would do really well at it."

Tara's breath caught in her throat. She wondered if this woman knew what had happened at her last job. She wondered if it was going to come around and bite her in the rear end if she didn't speak up. "Listen, I am very flattered, but I'm not sure if whoever you've been talking to told you what happened."

"Yes," she said interjecting, "and we understand how it is to work for Mack Valentine. He's not the easiest."

"True, but I still made some mistakes."

"Understandable, and we can talk about all of that if you'd like to set up a video interview."

Her breath caught in her throat. "Yes. Let's set that up. It never hurts to talk."

"Great. That's amazing news. I'll send you an email with more details of the job and some available times to video chat, but we're going to need your decision soon. We really want to fill the position within the next few weeks."

The next few weeks? That seemed awfully quick.

"I understand, and I'll get back to you as soon as I can with a time that we can do a video chat."

After she hung up, Tara sat there stunned. This job offer was truly her lifeline to her career in Atlanta. It was a chance to reclaim the path she thought she'd lost, but now Seagrove had become about so much more than just a refuge from her problems. It connected her with her past, with her grandmother, with her childhood, but most importantly, with Noah. The thought of leaving him just as they were finding each other again sent waves of sadness through her.

Could she really leave? She wasn't sure that she could. She decided not to tell Noah anything yet. She didn't want to upset him until she figured out what she was going to do. There was no need to burden him with her dilemma since she hadn't made up her mind. She closed her laptop, stood up and walked over to the window, staring out over the marsh. She felt so torn between two worlds. One was a world of professional fulfillment, the other a world of personal happiness. Could they coexist? Right now, it didn't seem like that was possible.

CHAPTER 10

*T*ara was so excited today that she got to go to the bookstore. She hadn't been to Down Yonder Bookstore in several years and she missed it. Nothing quite compared to the little independently owned bookstore in her hometown. Sure, she'd been to lots of big bookstores over the years, mostly chain ones back in the city, but this place held a special spot in her heart.

It had often been a refuge where she found solace among the stacks of books. She enjoyed the comforting aroma of coffee and the smell of the ink and paper as she walked in the door. It always smelled the same way in the bookstore, and it always came back to her when she visited. She could hear the soothing sound of jazz music playing in the background, and there were only a couple of other shoppers in the store.

She walked over to the front desk and asked the woman behind the counter for a cup of coffee before finding a quiet place to sit. She didn't recognize the woman, but her name tag said Meg.

"Are you new to town?" Meg asked her.

"Actually, no. I grew up here, but my grandmother recently passed away, so I came back to help settle her estate and ...," Tara stopped herself. And, what? She didn't know what came after settling the estate. Was she going to stay in Seagrove? It was a question that was constantly looming in her mind.

"Nice to meet you. I've been here for a few years myself. Just knew that I hadn't seen you before. So, I guess I don't need to welcome you to town," Meg said laughing.

"I've missed this place so much. Is Dixie around?"

"Actually, she just stepped out for a moment. She really doesn't work around here much anymore. My mother is owner of the store and she's typically working, but she's busy with some things right now."

"Oh, I had no idea that Dixie wasn't working."

"Well, you know she's getting a bit older and she's had some health issues, but recently she took up playing tennis."

Tara started laughing. "That sounds like Dixie. She's never going to let anything get her down."

"Who's not going to let anything get them down?" Dixie said, opening the door behind her with a big smile on her face. She still dressed just as flamboyantly as she always had. Today's ensemble was a pair of aqua blue capri pants with little pineapples embroidered all over them, a white T-shirt and a big gaudy necklace that had just about every color of the rainbow. Of course, her hair was still platinum blonde and was pulled up on top of her head today. She also had the biggest pair of red eyeglasses on. It all fit Dixie's personality. She was outgoing and was a typical Southern lady all at the same time.

"Hey, Dixie," Tara said walking over and hugging her tightly. Dixie had been one of her grandmother's best friends over the years. She'd heard lots of stories about them growing up.

"Tara, I cannot believe you're here. It's been so long since I've seen you," Dixie said. "I knew you'd come back to take care of your grandmother's house and all, but when she had opted not to have a memorial service, I wasn't sure if I'd see you."

"Yes, I'm staying at the house right now. Just trying to figure out what to do next."

"Well, don't you have to get back to the city? She told me all about your big job there."

Tara's face fell a bit. "I actually lost my job right before I found out that she passed away. Thankfully, she never knew."

"She was so proud of you no matter what, honey. Come over here and sit down and chat for a few minutes."

Tara took her cup of coffee and followed Dixie over to a table in the corner. "I just wanted to stay here for a bit just to clear my head. I'm not really sure what my future holds just yet."

"Boy, your grandmother sure will be missed in this town. She was a big part of everything that went on for so many years."

Tara nodded, sadness hanging in her heart. "She was amazing. I'll miss her every day for the rest of my life." They talked about her grandmother's legacy in Seagrove and how much everyone had loved her. Then Dixie said something that caught Tara completely off guard.

"You know, I was so impressed with that Noah."

"Really? You mean because of his artistic talent?" Tara said taking a sip of her coffee.

"Well that, and the fact that he was such a help to your grandmother in her final weeks. I mean, he was there just about every day. Every time I came to bring a casserole or a pot of soup, there was Noah sitting by her bedside, making sure she was comfortable and that she had everything she needed."

Tara felt like she couldn't breathe. She literally thought somebody might have to call an ambulance for her. She quickly swallowed the sip of coffee she had in her mouth just so she didn't choke on it. She looked at Dixie, shock obviously written across her face.

"Noah was taking care of her? I had no idea."

Dixie sensed Tara's surprise and probably wished she hadn't opened her mouth.

"I had no idea he didn't mention it, but yes, he was very diligent. He did such a good job for your grandmother. I know you must be thankful for that since you couldn't be here."

"I would've been here," Tara corrected her, "had I known anything about it. She wouldn't let anyone tell me, and he didn't tell me. I didn't even know she was ill. Why didn't at least Noah tell me?" she said out loud, speaking only to herself, really.

Dixie reached across the table and put a comforting hand over Tara's. "I'm sure that she swore him to secrecy, Tara. You know how stubborn she could be. She didn't want to burden you, I'm sure."

Her mind was racing. She felt a surge of anger that she hadn't felt in a very long time. She was hurt that Noah hadn't told her about her grandmother's condition, that he had kept this secret from her that caused her to never be able to say goodbye. Here she'd been at work living her life completely unaware that her grandmother was in her last moments, caught up in all her own troubles and being cared for by the man that she was now falling in love with, or truthfully, the man she'd been in love with since she was a child. And all these weeks, he didn't tell her anything about being with her grandmother. Her stomach churned.

She stood up abruptly, her chair scraping against the tile floor. "I'm sorry. I need to go, Dixie. Thanks for the chat."

She hurried out of the bookstore, her thoughts swirling in a turmoil. She felt so betrayed by Noah's silence. She didn't know what to think about any of it. She felt her face turning red with each passing moment. She knew she was going to have to confront him, but not right now. She was afraid of what she might say, what she might do. It certainly was casting a shadow of doubt over the trust and honesty that she thought they had in their relationship.

Julie was feeling like she was on cloud nine. She was practically floating as she got closer to the bookstore. She couldn't wait to share her news with Dixie and Meg, two of the most important women in her life. She walked to the door and opened it, hearing the familiar chime.

"I have some news!" she shouted out as soon as she opened the door, then realizing there might be customers in the store who would be startled by her antics. Thankfully, she didn't see any. Dixie looked up, her face in a wide smile.

"Julie, darlin', what's got you all bright-eyed?"

"I did it! I published my book. It's out there for the world to read," she said, shaking her hands in front of her chest like she was nervous.

Meg clapped her hands. "That's amazing, Mom! Congratulations."

Dixie walked around the counter and pulled her into a tight hug. "Well, Julie, that's wonderful, but you look as nervous as a long-tailed cat in a room full of rocking chairs. What's the matter?"

She sighed. "I'm just so nervous. What if it doesn't do well? What if people don't like it? I mean, everybody thinks their baby's the cutest, and some babies just aren't cute."

Dixie laughed and took Julie's hands. "Now, you listen here. You've put your heart and soul into that book. That alone is something to be proud of. Most people will never even get as far as you have. You remember that success ain't just about sales and numbers. It's about putting yourself out there and sharing a story from your heart. That will connect with somebody."

Meg nodded, "Mom, you've accomplished something incredible. You know how you've always told me and Colleen to follow our dreams? Well, you're living proof of that. You're who we look up to."

Dixie chimed in again, "Besides, you've always been a storyteller and now your story is out there in the big wide world. That is no small feat. You know what? People are going to love it. It might take a little time, but don't you dare belittle this achievement."

Julie felt like she was going to burst into tears at their encouragement.

"Thank you. Both of you. I guess I just needed to hear that."

"You're a part of this community, Julie. Everybody here is going to be rooting for you. We'll be right here as your personal cheerleading squad every step of the way."

As she poured herself a cup of coffee, her heart felt lighter. Dixie's words had given her a new perspective, as they always did. It wasn't really about how well her book sold. It was more about the journey and the courage that she had somehow summoned to not only write a book, but publish it. She knew she would always have the support of her family and friends, which meant that she could face whatever came next. Her story was out there, and that was a victory in and of itself.

Tara had never been so nervous in her life. Even when she was walking into Mack Valentine's office and about to get herself fired, she hadn't felt quite like this. These stakes felt so much higher to her. She had loved Noah since they were children, and the last few weeks had been some of the best of her life. She had never felt such a connection with someone and the words that she was about to say to him, and the outcome of this conversation, was also going to determine the outcome of their relationship. So yes, the stakes were way too high.

She had thought about walking home many times, but she knew herself well enough to know that she couldn't continue having this on her mind. Several hours had been long enough. She couldn't concentrate or think about anything else. And if she didn't talk to Noah about the deception, she definitely wouldn't sleep tonight.

She waited around outside of his art shop until he walked outside, locking the door behind him. When he turned around, she startled him.

"Tara, was I supposed to meet you tonight?"

"No, this is a bit unexpected," she said, pausing.

"Well, anytime I get to see you is a good time," he said, walking closer, about to touch her.

She stepped back. "We need to talk."

His brow furrowed with concern. "Of course. What's wrong?"

"It's about my grandmother," she said, trying to keep her voice steady. She wanted to burst into tears. "Today I found out that you took care of my grandmother in her last weeks, that you knew how sick she was and never told me."

His expression fell as he stared down at his shoes before looking back up at her. A mixture of sadness and possible regret washed over his face. "Tara, I…"

"Why, Noah?" she interrupted, her eyes filling

with tears. "Why didn't you tell me? You know how much I loved my grandmother? I had a right to know. I had a right to be here."

He sighed as he ran his hand through his hair. "I wanted to tell you. I really did. Your grandmother made me promise not to. She didn't want to burden you just like she said in the journal. She knew that you were busy at work, and she was so proud of you. And she just wanted you to remember her like she was, not as she became toward the end."

She shook her head, a bitter laugh escaping her lips. "So you decided to keep this huge secret from me even after she died? To make that choice on my behalf."

"Maybe I was protecting myself. Maybe it was selfish," he said, putting his hands in his pockets. "We were doing so well, and I didn't feel like you knowing that information was going to help things. It was going to make you mad at me and mad at your grandmother all over again."

"Well, I'm definitely mad at you right now," she said, gritting her teeth.

"I was so torn. Every day, I wanted to call you, but I couldn't break my promise to her. She was in such a bad way. If you had shown up, it probably would've broken her heart that you saw her like that."

She stepped back, distancing herself further. "I can't believe this, Noah. I just can't fathom how you could keep something like this from me. I trusted you and you deceived me, just like every other man in my life always has."

"Tara, please," he said, pleading with her. "I'm sorry. I didn't mean to hurt you or deceive you. I thought I was doing the right thing in a very difficult situation. I knew that you would want someone there to take care of your grandmother. So, I stepped up. I made sure that her last moments were as peaceful as they could be. I coordinated food deliveries from the community. I made sure that her pastor was there. I made sure that she had a home health aide that she liked. I slept there so many nights."

"I appreciate all of that," Tara said. "I really do. Thank you for taking care of her. But that doesn't negate the fact that we were best friends our entire lives and you didn't tell me. You didn't trust me enough with the information, even after the fact."

He stepped forward again, touching her on the arm, and she pulled away.

"How can I fix this? I don't know what to do."

"I don't know what to think right now, Noah. I feel so betrayed. I had weeks to see my grandmother, and I wasn't here because you kept me in the dark."

His eyes were filled with pain, which made her feel terrible, but she was just too angry to care. There was a part of her that knew she was letting her anger and hurt cloud her judgment and choose her words, but she couldn't muster the energy to care. She just wanted to lash out.

"I need time. I need to figure out what to do about this and how I feel. I'm not sure about us right now."

"Don't let this be the end of us," Noah said. "We've worked so hard to get here. I don't want to lose you all over again."

She turned away and started walking toward home. "I need to be alone," she called back over her shoulder just in case he was thinking of following her.

The sound of her footsteps echoed as she walked down the sidewalk before she turned for home. She wanted to run all the way back to the house and fall onto the sofa in a heap, and maybe that was just what she would do.

There was nothing better than a summer barbecue in the South Carolina Lowcountry. Julie and Dawson's home was abuzz with excitement as the smell of barbecue wafted through the air in their backyard overlooking the ocean.

Dawson was busy at the grill making ribs and barbecued chicken, while several of the women were coming in and out of the house with delectable dishes like potato salad, baked beans, and peach cobbler for dessert.

Today was a celebration. It was more than just a family cookout. They were celebrating Julie's newly launched author career and the beginning of her new journey. As she stood beside Dawson, watching him monitor the food, her heart was full of joy. She thought about how her life had been just several years ago. How she'd been in a broken marriage, living in a place where her friends really weren't her friends. She had no idea what she was missing all those years, but she was thankful that her life had to break apart so that she could rebuild it even better.

She remembered hearing years ago that there was a type of Japanese pottery that involved taking broken pieces and putting them back together with gold. That's exactly how she thought of her own life. Everything had broken apart several years ago, and she thought it was over, but God put everything back together with gold, and now her life was stronger than ever. Now she had a community around her that made her feel supported and loved.

She never worried that one day she would be alone as many people her age did. She had both of her daughters and her son. She had her two new grandchildren, and of course she had her wonderful husband. She was surrounded by her mother, her sister, and her new best friends. There was nothing that she didn't have. Being a published author was really just the cherry on top of a life that was almost hard to believe.

Everybody kept coming up and congratulating her, which made her feel full of pride. Just completing a book had been such a big obstacle. Then sending it off, then getting rejected, and then finally publishing it herself. It felt very much like the power she took back after her divorce. She was tired of allowing everybody around her to control how she lived her life, and she had arrived in Seagrove feeling very much broken. Now she was built back better than ever, full of veins of gold.

She had a few copies of her paperback book

lying on a table, so everybody kept walking over and picking them up.

"Mom, this is incredible. Look at you, Miss Published Author," Colleen said, hugging her tightly. She held baby Deacon in her arms, and even he looked like he was smiling at her.

"We're so proud of you. You're an inspiration to all of us," Meg said.

She was so thankful to have two grown daughters who had really become more like best friends. Sure, they'd had their issues throughout the years when they were teenagers and just into college, but now they were strong women, mothers themselves, and she was so proud of them.

"Thank you, my loves. I couldn't have done any of this without everybody's support, including yours. Just seeing my book in print is so exciting. That alone is a dream come true."

Dawson overheard them talking and picked up his glass of sweet tea. "I propose a toast," he said to everyone standing around, which included Dixie and Janine. "To Julie, whose perseverance and talent have shown us that it's never too late to chase your dreams. Cheers."

Everybody held up their glasses and yelled "Cheers", and she savored that moment of triumph and togetherness with the people she loved most in the world.

"Congratulations, Julie. The book looks great," William said, walking over and hugging her.

"I agree. I love this cover and it looks really professional inside," Tucker said. She took that as high praise coming from such a great businessman.

"And we all know it's going to be a big hit," Dixie yelled from across the way, holding up her glass of sweet tea.

As the sun set, Julie felt such a sense of gratitude. Her journey had not been easy, but it had taught her more about resilience and how strong she was than anything else. It taught her the power of dreaming at any age and the unbreakable bond of family and friends. She knew her heart and mind were full of stories that were yet to be told and adventures in her life that were yet to be lived. Today was not just a celebration of a book, it was a celebration of a brand new life that only kept getting better and better.

CHAPTER 11

Tara had spent days thinking about the job opportunity that had been offered to her. She didn't really know what she wanted to do because she was so full of emotion after finding out what Noah had done. She didn't want to make a rash decision, but the offer was only good for a short period.

Her heart pounded with a mix of dread and determination as she walked again towards Noah's shop. He'd tried to text her and call her a few times, but she had made it very clear that she wanted him to stop, to give her time to think. All it did was give her time to miss him. But she couldn't think about that right now. She'd already had to make some hard decisions.

In a few weeks, she would sell her grandmother's

house and the land. She wasn't going to be coming back to Seagrove. She was going back to Atlanta to pursue her career and try to forget this whole thing, try to forget that she'd lost the woman who was a mother to her, try to forget that there was no place else on earth like Seagrove, but most of all, try to forget that she was madly in love with somebody who had lied to her. She just needed to cut bait and run, as they said.

That morning, she had emailed and accepted the job in Atlanta. It had been one of the hardest decisions she'd ever made. She had also called a real estate agent in Seagrove to set the ball rolling on selling the house and the land. Now, all that was left was to break the news to Noah. She stood outside the door of the shop, taking a deep breath, trying to steady herself, and then she pushed the door open.

He was at his workbench in the side room, his hands trying to assemble a beautiful sea glass mosaic. He looked up, his face first lighting up with a smile that faltered when he saw her very serious expression.

"Tara, I'm glad you came. Does this mean that you forgive me?" he said, with a hopeful smile on his face. She hesitated, trying to figure out the right words.

"I just needed to come here and tell you something. I got a job offer a few days ago."

"Well, that's great, Tara. Congratulations."

"It's in Atlanta." He stalled for a moment and just stood there, his face slightly falling. He knew what that meant. "I wasn't sure what to do about it, but I made the decision to take it."

He walked toward her. "Wait, so you're leaving?"

"Yes. I have already talked to a real estate agent about selling the house and the land."

His eyes widened. "You're selling your grandmother's house?"

"Yes. There's really no reason to keep it if I'm not going to be living here."

"Tara, please tell me this isn't because of what happened with your grandmother. Because I didn't tell you about her illness?"

"While that is part of it, to be honest, the only thing that would've been holding me here to Seagrove was the possibility of a relationship with you. I don't feel like that is something I want to pursue now."

"I don't understand it. You're talking to me like we barely know each other. I'm your best friend."

"You were my best friend when we were kids. I think it was silly to think that we could just suddenly make a romantic relationship out of that as adults. Either way, what happened made me question things between us. It's not just about that. This job is a chance to rebuild the career that I've worked so hard for. I can't just give that up because of the possibility that I could date you."

Again, he ran his hand through his hair. "I get it about the job, Tara, but I thought we were moving past this secret. I thought you would get over it and I could apologize and we could work through it together."

"Well, I guess you thought wrong," she said.

"So, that's it. It's over? There's no chance for us to be together?"

"I had hoped we could," she said, "but it's all just too complicated now. Between feeling the loss of my grandmother and having this job possibility, I just need to do what's best for me right now, Noah."

He walked closer and put his hands on her upper arms, making her feel like she just wanted to slide in and hug him tightly. That would be the easy thing to do.

"I get it, and I don't want to ever hold you back from your dreams, but I thought we had something special."

"I thought we did, too," she whispered, trying not

to make eye contact. "But for once, I need to put myself first. I need to be alone, I think." Even as she said the words, she knew she was lying through her teeth. She needed and wanted to be with Noah more than she needed or wanted her next breath. But making the jump to trusting him and fully giving up her career in Atlanta was just too hard. She wasn't brave enough or strong enough, she supposed.

There was a heavy silence between them for a while before he stepped back, nodding slowly.

"I can't stop you from leaving, and I wouldn't even if I could, because all I ever wanted was for you to be happy, even if that meant we had to be apart. That's why I took care of your grandmother. Just so you would always know that she was well taken care of at the end, even if you didn't know it was me."

"Thank you for taking care of her. I really do appreciate that more than you'll ever know. You'll always mean so much to me. We have great memories together."

He didn't say anything else. He just stared at her with a long, lingering look, before she finally turned and left the shop, the bell ringing behind her, hollow in her ears. Her heart felt just as hollow.

As she walked away, her heart had never felt heavier in her life. She wasn't just leaving him behind. She was leaving behind Seagrove, her childhood, her grandmother, and even a part of herself. Even as she made that decision and started walking toward the new opportunity that awaited her in Atlanta, she worried that she had made the wrong choice.

Almost three weeks had passed since Tara took the new job in Atlanta. It was kind of hard getting used to being in the city again. She had spoken to the real estate agent a couple of times about the house and the land. It was almost ready to be put on the market after making just a few minor repairs to the house. In fact, the real estate agent would be sending her the papers to sign any day now. Once she signed, it would go on the market for the first time ever. What would her grandmother think if she knew?

That reminded her that she needed to check her email when she got home from work. As she walked the busy Atlanta streets heading back after lunch, she felt conflicting emotions just like she'd felt every day since she left Seagrove. That conversation with Noah had been the last one. She hadn't gone back to see him. She hadn't returned his texts or phone calls. She just couldn't take saying goodbye again, or him trying to talk her out of it. Every day at work, she found herself thinking about him.

She would have to bring herself back to reality in an effort not to mess up another story. The last thing she needed was to get fired again and have that on her resume. But the truth was she absolutely hated being a staff reporter. It felt very much beneath what she had been doing before. She had been much higher up the chain of command and doing something she enjoyed, and she really hadn't understood what this job entailed more than just getting her out of Seagrove and away from Noah.

Her boss was a little bit demanding and sent her out on stories that bored her to tears. She wasn't writing what she wanted to write; she wasn't asking the questions she wanted to ask, and more importantly, she wasn't even living where she wanted to live. She found herself thinking about Noah's eyes crinkling when he smiled, or the warmth of his hand when it covered hers. Sometimes she swore she could hear his laughter mixing with the ocean breeze as it had for most of their lives.

In her mind, she saw his art shop, the shelves all lined with intricate sea glass creations. She smelled the salty sea air. She thought about the afternoons that she spent watching him work, completely absorbed in his craft, his focus only broken by the smiles he would throw her way. These moments that she'd had just for those few weeks felt like treasured gifts from a long ago life. She thought about their last conversations, the words that she'd said that she wished she hadn't, and the words that she wished she had said.

She had thought a lot about forgiveness and about her grandmother's last days, and how comforting it must have been to have Noah with her. Noah's presence comforted Tara after all, and there wouldn't have been anyone that she would've trusted more with her grandmother. She knew he was sorry for not telling her, and she wondered so many times if she had been too hasty walking away. Too quick to let her anger and hurt cloud the deep connection that they had shared their whole lives.

In her darkest moments, she thought about the next woman that came along and realized what a prize Noah really was. The woman who would take her place and edge her out of his heart. The woman who would hold his hand. The woman who would press her cheek to his chest and sway with the music under the Lowcountry starry nights to come. The woman who would slip a ring on his finger and call him her husband. It made her feel nauseous.

The more she thought about it, the more she questioned her decision to leave. The more she forced herself to get up and go to work each day, the more she realized what it would take for her to actually sign those real estate papers. Had she traded her one chance at true happiness for this career that now seemed unfulfilling? Had her grandmother written so much about her first love in that journal just to remind Tara that Noah was hers?

Had her pursuit of professional redemption caused her to lose the very thing that would make her happy? Love, stability, her hometown community? She remembered the way that Noah looked at her, the way he truly saw her and understood her in a way that no one else did. She felt comfort in his presence like she was coming home, and she realized how precious and rare that was as she stood out on the sidewalk in front of her workplace, looking around at all the people buzzing about. She had found not just a connection to her past, but the connection to her future in Noah.

With the endless stream of cars and constant buzz of city life, she saw how easy it was for people to be disconnected. And now that she had been reconnected to Seagrove and to Noah, she felt like she was an alien standing on a city street. She missed the simplicity of life in Seagrove, the ease of how days could be spent surrounded by people and nature. When she finally reached the office and walked inside, she felt lonely. There were people all around, but she didn't feel a connection to them.

The walls were devoid of personal touches and seemed to close in on her. She felt like she might be having a panic attack. In that moment, she longed for the comfort of her grandmother's house, for those long evenings spent with Noah and for the sense of belonging that she had only ever felt in Seagrove. When she finally got home that night from work, she was lying in her bed, staring at the ceiling, looking at the shadows dancing in the faint light of the city. Her thoughts were all-consuming, and she felt so far away from what she really wanted. Like her heart was beating somewhere outside of her chest.

But what could she do? She had already set the wheels in motion for selling the house and the land. She had already taken a job and started working. And she had already ended things with Noah. He probably didn't even feel the same way about her anymore. In the quiet of the night, she curled up in her blanket, a tear streaming down her cheek as she admitted to herself that she missed him more than she would ever allow herself to acknowledge out loud.

She missed his voice and his touch. She missed how he understood her better than she understood herself, but more than anything, she missed the possibility of what things could have become. She kicked herself for walking away from something that was truly special. When she finally fell asleep, the last thought she had was that she would dream of him and that she would feel peace when she woke up in the morning, even though that was probably impossible. She had literally made her bed and now had to lie in it.

She couldn't believe she was standing here. The warm sun beat down on her in the early morning hours as her feet dug into the sand. He hadn't seen her yet. The sun was just starting to cast a golden light on the beach as she saw him walking along the shoreline, his eyes doing what they always did - scanning the sand for pieces of sea glass, for treasures that he could make into beautiful pieces of art.

The waves were crashing gently against the shore, a soothing melody, something she had missed for the last several weeks. He was lost in his thoughts, not even noticing her standing there on the other side of the beach. Nothing had felt better than driving into Seagrove. She'd come in the night before, but she didn't want to go to see Noah until this morning. After all, the place that she felt was best to talk to him was right there on *their* beach, the place they had been millions of times it seemed.

She saw him bend down to pick up a frosted piece of blue glass, and that's when he noticed her. He froze in place for a moment before finally turning his head and looking at her. She took a step forward, cutting the distance in two.

"Noah," she called out softly. He straightened up, the piece of sea glass forgotten in his hand. He stared at her like she was an apparition.

"Tara? What are you doing here?" She walked closer, her steps slow because she didn't know how he felt.

"I came back," she said nervously.

He looked tentative. She couldn't quite read the

expression on his face. "You're back? For how long? Just to close on the house?"

She took a deep breath, gathering up all the courage she could. "No, I'm back for good. I realized something when I was in Atlanta."

"Oh, yeah? What was that?" he said, putting the piece of sea glass in his pocket.

"I realized that leaving Seagrove, and leaving you, was the biggest mistake I've ever made."

His expression softened. "I don't understand. Why did you come back?"

"I guess I had to go back to Atlanta just to see how much I would miss you. Miss this place," she said. "I am selling that land that my grandmother left me because I'm going to start my own online show focusing on Lowcountry beach living. This is where I belong, Noah. Here, with you, if you'll still have me."

The initial awkwardness between them started to dissipate like a heavy fog. It was replaced by a growing sense of hope in Tara's heart. He stepped closer, only inches between them.

"Tara, are you sure about this? I don't want you to have any regrets, and I don't want you to hold resentment to me for taking care of your grandmother and not telling you."

Her eyes met his. "I've never been more sure about anything in my life. I've missed you more than I thought I could ever possibly miss someone, and I'm sorry that I reacted that way about my grandmother. Looking back, I know that she was trying to protect me, and she was a stubborn old lady who probably forced you into making that promise."

He laughed. "She was stubborn. And a little scary."

"I know that you did everything you could for her, and I'm eternally grateful for that. I think I just needed to work through those feelings instead of running away. But the question is, do you still want to be with me?"

"Of course I want to be with you. I've missed you, Tara, so much," he said, his voice thick with emotion. He reached out, his hand gently cupping her face. Their eyes locked, and he slowly leaned in, pressing his lips to hers. It was a kiss that felt more like a new beginning than a reunion. It spoke of missed opportunities and second chances.

As they finally pulled away and the sun was rising higher in the sky, Tara looked up at him, smiling. "I'm home, Noah."

"And I'm here for you. Always," he said, his voice filled with love and contentment. They stood there on the beach, hand in hand, watching the sun rise all the way into the sky, looking out on a new chapter of both of their lives. Tara didn't feel uncertain. She knew whatever happened, they would face it together because their love was an anchor that had grounded them since they were little kids.

EPILOGUE

*T*ara sat on the porch of her house, which she had stopped calling her grandmother's home and finally started calling her own. She had done a little redecorating over the last few months trying to make it into something that she would like as she grew her family over time.

It was a charming little home, filled with memories and warmth, and it was hers now. A place where she had started a new chapter. She looked out at the garden, a smile on her lips, her laptop opened in front of her. She was so proud of the latest edition of her online show. It had become a resounding success, a vibrant celebration of coastal life, culture, and the unique charm of the Lowcountry. She was so proud of this place that she'd come from that she had wanted to share it with the world. Advertisers had flocked to her new show, and now she was going to be expanding into a podcast and possibly even a magazine.

She hadn't quite figured out how to do all of that yet, but she knew that she could bring her passion to the stories and connect with readers who had a love for this area of the country. Finally, her work felt like it was important. It didn't have to be some big, fancy TV show in the city to touch people and change their lives. Her decision to finally get out of the city and not go back hadn't been a hard one in the end. What was surprising was that Mack Valentine had reached out to her many months later with an offer to allow her to return to the TV show where she had worked. She knew Seagrove and Noah were both where she belonged, and that her business venture was more than just a job; it was now a part of her. So she had quickly declined, thanking him for the opportunity. She heard Noah's footsteps on the porch outside, which pulled her from her thoughts.

He walked over with an easy smile holding two cups of coffee. "I thought you might need a refill", he said handing her a cup.

"Thanks," Tara said, taking the coffee from his hands. "I'm just finishing up some work. You know the show has really been taking off."

"I'm not surprised. You've got a talent for telling stories that matter," Noah said. "And everybody can now see the beautiful South Carolina Lowcountry through your eyes."

They sat together on this peaceful evening, and then Tara turned to Noah, her eyes reflecting in the soft porch light.

"You know I sold the land today. The deal is final."

"That's wonderful. I know it wasn't an easy decision, but I know that it's the money that you need to keep building your new business."

"It wasn't easy, but it feels right. I know it's what my grandmother would've wanted me to do, and now it gives me the financial freedom to focus on what I love, and on us"" she said, her hand finding Noah's.

"Plus, who knows who's going to buy the land. Maybe an interesting new person will arrive in Seagrove and do something great with it." His fingers laced with hers. "I'm here for whatever our future holds, Tara. We sure have come a long way since we were kids, haven't we?"

"We have," she said, resting her head on his shoulder. "And I think where we're going is going to be equally as wonderful."

They looked out at the stars that were just beginning to twinkle in the night sky over the marsh, and the possibilities of the future stretched out before them just like the endless ocean. These two people who were connected by a shared past and looking forward to a shared future also got to share the beauty of Seagrove every day together as they built their life. And Tara couldn't be more thankful for everything her grandmother had put in place to make sure that she got to live out her dream with her first love, even though her grandmother didn't.

J ulie stood behind the counter at Down Yonder Bookstore, looking over at the small poster on the wall that was announcing her next book signing event. She had been so shocked at how well her first book had done. Certainly, she wasn't going to hit any bestseller lists or be able to retire tomorrow, but the book had sold well, much better than expected. The funny thing was she had heard back from a publisher after her book was self-published, and they had wanted to take a look at it, let her know what they thought, and possibly publish it for her. She had to let them down and tell them that she had already done it herself and planned to continue that way.

That first book had been such a labor of love that had taken years to come to fruition. Now, she was writing her second one, and it was gratifying to know that she had readers waiting to read it. Her book had found a special place in the hearts of the community of Seagrove and beyond, and now she was going to be doing more book signings in surrounding towns.

As she prepared to publish her second book, she felt a sense of excitement. Writing had just started as a hobby, a way to channel her creativity and share her stories, but now it had turned into something more; a way to connect with other people to share in their experiences and to bring them peace and joy in hard times when they needed to escape into the pages of the book.

The chime on the door announced a customer walking in, so Julie brought herself back into the present moment. She greeted the person with her usual warm smile and helped them find the perfect book. Between customers, she always worked on finalizing the details of her upcoming signing or worked on the editing of her current book. The success of her writing had brought such a new dimension to her life. She wasn't in it for the fame or fortune. After all, it was a very hard and lonely job at times. She wanted it to be something that helped others. And the extra income was just a welcome bonus. It allowed her to occasionally spoil her grandchildren and put some money into their college accounts, and of course, to add some money to her own retirement account.

There was nothing better than working in a bookstore and being an author, she had decided. It was the community hub, a place where stories lived and breathed every day, and now her own stories were a part of that very tapestry. As she locked up the store for that night and walked outside, she thought about just what a fulfilling life it was to get to tell stories and make other people happy. As she strolled under the starlit Seagrove sky, she knew she had found her calling in so many ways; mother, entrepreneur, author, wife. Everything had come into fruition that she had dreamed of her entire life. She just had to be willing to allow everything to break apart for it to come together even more beautifully than she could have ever imagined.

This series is an ongoing series, so there will be more books coming! If you'd like to be notified, be sure to join Rachel's very active Facebook community by going to https://www.facebook.com/groups/RachelReaders.

To see a list of all of Rachel's books and find out about the best deals, visit store.RachelHannaAuthor.com.